BRODY

BRODY

TEXAS BOUDREAU BROTHERHOOD

By

KATHY IVAN

COPYRIGHT

BRODY – Texas Boudreau Brotherhood

While local Fire Chief Brody Boudreau has his hands full with a series of suspected arsons plaguing his small town of Shiloh Springs, he finds it impossible to stop thinking about its newest resident. When Beth Stewart's ex-husband escapes from behind bars and threatens her and her young daughter, can Brody protect the woman he's come to love, or will he lose his chance at happiness before it even begins?

BOOKS BY KATHY IVAN

www.kathyivan.com/books.html

TEXAS BOUDREAU BROTHERHOOD

Rafe

Antonio

Brody

NEW ORLEANS CONNECTION SERIES

Desperate Choices

Connor's Gamble

Relentless Pursuit

Ultimate Betrayal

Keeping Secrets

Sex, Lies and Apple Pies

Deadly Justice

Wicked Obsession

Hidden Agenda

Spies Like Us

Fatal Intentions

New Orleans Connection Series Box Set: Books 1-3

New Orleans Connection Series Box Set: Books 4-7

CAJUN CONNECTION SERIES

Saving Sarah

Saving Savannah

Saving Stephanie

Guarding Gabi

Dear Reader,

Welcome to Shiloh Springs, Texas! Don't you just love a small Texas town, where the people are neighborly, the gossip plentiful, and the heroes are …well, heroic, not to mention easy on the eyes! I love everything about Texas, which I why I've made the great state my home for over thirty years. There's no other place like it. From the delicious Tex-Mex food and downhome barbecue, the majestic scenery, and friendly atmosphere, the people and places of the Lone Star state are as unique and colorful as you'll find anywhere.

The Texas Boudreau Brotherhood series centers around a group of foster brothers, men who would have ended up in the system if not for Douglas and Patricia Boudreau. Instead of being hardened by life and circumstances beyond their control, they found a family who loved and accepted them, and gave them a place to call home. Sometimes brotherhood is more than sharing the same DNA.

If you've read my other romantic suspense books (the New Orleans Connection series and Cajun Connection series), you'll be familiar with the Boudreau name. Turns out there are a whole lot of Boudreaus out there, just itching to have their stories told. (Douglas is the brother of Gator Boudreau, patriarch of the New Orleans branch of the Boudreau family.)

So, sit back and relax. The pace of small-living might be less hectic than the big city, but small towns hold secrets, excitement, and heroes to ride to the rescue. And who doesn't love a Texas cowboy?

Kathy Ivan

EDITORIAL REVIEWS

"Kathy Ivan's books are addictive, you can't read just one."

—Susan Stoker, NYT Bestselling Author

"Kathy Ivan's books give you everything you're looking for and so much more."

—Geri Foster, USA Today and NYT Bestselling Author of the Falcon Securities Series

"In Shiloh Springs, Kathy Ivan has crafted warm, engaging characters that will steal your heart and a mystery that will keep you reading to the very last page."

—Barb Han, *USA TODAY* and Publisher's Weekly Bestselling Author

"This is the first I have read from Kathy Ivan and it won't be the last."

—Night Owl Reviews

"I highly recommend Desperate Choices. Readers can't go wrong here!"

—Melissa, Joyfully Reviewed

"I loved how the author wove a very intricate storyline with plenty of intriguing details that led to the final reveal…"

—Night Owl Reviews

Desperate Choices—Winner 2012 International Digital Award—Suspense

Desperate Choices—Best of Romance 2011 –Joyfully Reviewed

DEDICATIONS AND ACKNOWLEDGEMENTS

A special shout out to all the readers who keep me going. Knowing you enjoy my books and want more, I have to admit there's no greater feeling in the world. To my sister, Mary. She is always there, helping me, encouraging me, and generally doing whatever it takes to get the writing done. Trust me, if she wasn't there prodding me, the books might never be finished. And, as always, I dedicate every book to my mother, Betty Sullivan. She loved reading and shared that love for books with me at a young age. She instilled in me the joy of reading from an early age and a love of romance. Her belief in happily ever after keeps me writing.

More about Kathy and her books can be found at

WEBSITE:
www.kathyivan.com

Follow Kathy on Facebook at
www.facebook.com/kathyivanauthor

Follow Kathy on Twitter at
twitter.com/@kathyivan

Follow Kathy at BookBub
bookbub.com/profile/kathy-ivan

NEWSLETTER SIGN UP

Don't want to miss out on any new books, contests, and free stuff? Sign up to get my newsletter. I promise not to spam you, and only send out notifications/e-mails whenever there's a new release or contest/giveaway. Follow the link and join today!

http://eepurl.com/baqdRX

BRODY

By
KATHY IVAN

CHAPTER ONE

Watching the last smoldering board collapse onto the darkened, scorched earth, Brody Boudreau felt a growing weariness deep in his bones. This fire had burned hotter than an inferno. Hotter than a normal fire. His suspicion? It had been intentionally set. He'd wait until things cooled down enough to start a formal investigation, but his gut told him an accelerant aided in the destruction of the deserted old barn.

The only bright spot in an otherwise hellish night was the building had been abandoned years ago. Once a decent-sized working barn, now it was little more than a large empty structure. The aged and dry wood would have sparked like a rocket under normal circumstances. But this? Surveying the path of destruction leading away from the barn more than likely would prove to be gasoline, maybe kerosene.

Were there spontaneous fires in Shiloh Springs? Of course, especially when it had been hot and dry throughout a good chunk of the past couple of years. There'd been little rain this summer, and while they weren't in official drought conditions, the whole county was pretty darn close. Add in

Texas' one hundred plus degree days and you had the makings of a perfect storm.

He might have chalked this up to local teens, sneaking around, smoking and getting high, if this was the first building to go up in flames. Nope, it was the fourth in as many months, a distinct pattern as far as he was concerned. They'd been lucky so far, nobody got hurt, but it was only a matter of time before somebody got careless.

Time to nip it in the bud before things got worse.

"What do ya think, Brody?" Dwayne, one of the volunteer firefighters who'd shown up to help, stood beside him, sweat pouring down his face. Streaks of black soot covered his skin and hair, and he swiped a sweaty forearm across his brow. "Personally, I think we've got a firebug on our hands."

"Hate to say it, but you might be right." Brody pointed to the charred path leading toward the collapsed structure. "My guess? Looks like somebody used an accelerant. We'll know more once we can get inside and check things out."

"You gonna tell the sheriff?"

Brody nodded, shoulders slumped. "Don't see I've got much choice. Too much of a coincidence having this many spontaneous fires break out. All at unoccupied properties or abandoned sites like this one."

"I think we're about ready to head back to the station. Need a lift?"

"Thanks, I've got my truck. I'm going to head over to the sheriff's office, then try to grab a couple hours' shut eye.

Tell the guys I'll talk to them later. Appreciate their hard work. They did a great job."

"Sure thing, Chief."

Dwayne walked away, helmet under his arm, to the fire truck where the others were checking the equipment and reloading it for the return trip. Brody was proud of his guys, men and women who worked tirelessly when called upon. Tonight had been no exception. They'd worked and trained, making sure they maintained a ready status for nights like this, and they'd done an exceptional job, and he'd make sure they knew how much they were valued and appreciated.

With a weary sigh, he climbed behind the wheel of his pickup and headed into Shiloh Springs proper, pulling up in front of the sheriff's station. It was early, but he spotted his brother's car parked a few yards up the street. Though barely light outside, he wasn't surprised his big brother was already in the office. In his opinion, Rafe was the finest sheriff Shiloh Springs ever had, and he worked harder than anybody to make sure the folks in his county felt safe. Too bad the news Brody brought might chuck a spanner in the works.

He jumped at the loud knock on his window. His brother Chance stood outside. Rolling the window down, he scrubbed a hand over his face, noting the smoky, charred scent. *Probably should have showered before heading here.*

"Anything wrong?"

"Another fire, this time at the abandoned Summers' place. It's out now, but the barn is a total loss."

"That's what, the fourth one?"

Brody nodded and climbed out of the car. "Yeah. Decided to stop off and talk with Rafe, update him on what's happening, before I head home and try and grab a couple hours' shut eye. Probably could have slept at the station, but I need some time to clear my head."

"I'm heading in to see Rafe too. Mind if I sit in?"

"Sure, I'd welcome your input, Mr. District Attorney. You're gonna hear all about it anyway, might as well update you both on what we've found."

Chance held the door open, and they headed back toward Rafe's office. The rest of the office seemed empty, though it wouldn't be for long. Soon there'd be deputies dealing with the daily grind of small-town crimes. Sally Anne covered dispatch, along with most of the clerical work, because dispatch for the Shiloh Springs sheriff's department wasn't a high demand occupation. Most times, folks' problems got solved without anybody ever leaving the office.

Rafe sat behind his desk, a stack of folders hovering near the edge, a tricky balancing act. One good gust of wind and the leaning tower would topple over, spilling papers everywhere. He glanced up as Brody and Chance walked in, and tossed his pen onto the desk. "Morning. Why didn't you bring coffee?"

"Good morning to you too, grouch. I'd planned on inviting you to breakfast at Daisy's, but since you're in a foul mood…"

"Sorry, Chance. I hate paperwork, and these new state requirements are making things worse. Nowadays, if somebody sneezes inside a cell, we have to write up a report and send it to half a dozen agencies. It's beginning to look like I can't get anything done except deal with bureaucracy. I didn't sign up for this. But, that's my headache. What brings you guys by this early?"

"Let Brody go first. He's been up all night."

Rafe's eyes narrowed, taking in everything with that perceptive cop stare he'd perfected, and Brody rolled his eyes. Great, now big brother was going to go into protective mode, like he'd always done even when they were kids. Rafe's protective streak was a mile wide, and he had the compassionate heart to match. There wasn't anything wrong with him a shower and some uninterrupted sleep wouldn't fix. *At least nothing physical.*

"We had another fire last night." Brody ease onto the chair across from Rafe's desk, and Chance slid onto the other. "I hate to say this, but I think we've got a problem."

"You suspect arson?"

Brody nodded, and ran a hand through his hair. He felt filthy, coated in layers of grime and soot. He was used to it, a part of the job he loved, yet even the thought of somebody deliberately starting fires in his county, close to the people he cared about, made him feel dirty. And pissed off.

"Wasn't hard to spot. I found what I believe is clear evidence of an accelerant. I've collected a ton of evidence at the scene, and once things cool off, and it's not pitch dark outside, I'll take a closer look. But with three other fires this close together, there's a definitive pattern."

"That's what now, four?"

"In the last few months, yeah. Another part of the pattern I'm seeing is the fires have all been in abandoned or vacant properties. This one was at the old Summers' barn. It's been empty for years, it's outside of town, the wood is old and dried out, making it a firebug's dream spot."

"Plus, it's off the beaten path. Unless you know it's there, it's not visible from the road. Add in the use of an accelerant, you're right, sounds suspicious." Rafe scratched at his chin while he watched Brody closely. Brody was used to his big brother's scrutiny. He really should have stopped and showered first, because knowing Rafe, he wasn't going to pass up the opportunity to rib him about trailing smoke into the sanctity of his office.

"Unofficially, I wanted to give you a head's up. I'll send you an official report once I've had a chance to do a more thorough investigation. Collect more samples for ILRs and send then for testing."

"I probably know this, but I'm drawing a blank. What's ILRs?" Chance shook his head after asking the question. "Guess Rafe's not the only one needing some coffee."

"ILRs is an ignitable liquid residue. Not necessarily an accelerant, but burns hot. Most likely I'll find gasoline or kerosene. Maybe propane, but I doubt it. I'll also check for pour patterns, if an accelerant was used. Thought I spotted some after the fire was out."

"I'll have my deputies keep their eyes peeled for anybody acting weird. I haven't heard of any strangers passing through. I'll keep you posted if I hear anything."

Brody stood up and stretched. "Appreciate it. I'm heading to the Big House. I'll crash there for a few hours and then head back to the scene. Call me if anything comes up."

"Will do. Get some rest, you've earned it."

Chance also stood and headed for the door. "I'm going to head out too, since you've got your hands full, bro. Might as well head in to the office and get some work done. I'll update you later on a couple of cases."

"Before you go, have you heard anything more about the Berkley case? Antonio's swamped between moving back from Dallas, and getting situated at his new digs with the Austin FBI office. I didn't want to bring it up with Serena; she's been through enough already."

Brody paused halfway to the door, because he wanted to hear the answer too, since that particular case had hit a little too close to home. Although it did have a bright side. His brother, Antonio, found the love of his life during the whole fiasco. A few weeks prior, Big Jim Berkley, homegrown terrorist and the mastermind behind several bombings across the southern United States, had been granted an appeal of his conviction. The one person who could keep him behind bars was the man's niece, who'd been living in Shiloh

Springs under an assumed identity. Fortunately, things turned out the way they should, and Antonio and Serena got their happily ever after. Brody suspected there'd be wedding bells in the near future for his brother. The thought made him smile.

"The Department of Justice quietly steamrollered him into taking an Alford plea on all the new charges. There won't be another trial. Big Jim Berkley's new attorneys agreed to withdraw their case for appeal. Big Jim's never gonna see the outside of a penitentiary for the rest of his natural life." Chance shrugged. "Couldn't have happened to a better person. With everything he put Serena through, they should bury him beneath the jail. That's my personal opinion. As the district attorney for the county of Shiloh Springs, I cannot quote anything on the record, since there are still charges pending against Jonathan and Corinne Drury for the auto accident and attempted kidnapping of Serena."

"Are you prosecuting their case?"

"I can't, Brody. I've recused myself, since my brothers were involved and will be called as witnesses for the prosecution. Don't want anything smacking of nepotism or impropriety to taint the case. Off the record, they'll probably plead it out, since both Drury and his wife have charges pending in an ongoing investigation with the Justice Department. Shiloh Springs is small potatoes in their ongoing case."

"I'm glad Antonio's moving back. I think Shiloh Springs is good for his soul. In the short time he's been back, he seems, I don't know, happier."

Rafe chuckled. "Well, part of that might be because he's in love. I know I'm certainly happier now I've got Tessa in my life."

"And with that, I'm out of here, in case all this new love stuff is contagious. I am not ready to settle down." With a grin, Chance walked out of Rafe's office, whistling as he headed toward the front. Brody heard him greet Sally Anne, who must've come in while they'd been talking.

"I'm out too."

As he turned to go, Rafe placed a hand on his arm. "Bro, are you alright? I don't want to pry, but you haven't been yourself for a while. Anything I can do to help?"

Brody drew in a deep breath. He thought they hadn't noticed, but trust his big brother to strike right at the heart of the matter. How was he supposed to tell Rafe he'd fallen for his fiancée's sister? The one who'd be Rafe's sister-in-law before too long?

"Everything's fine. I'm just tired. Burning the candle at both ends; guess it's caught up to me. I've finished up the latest classes for TCFP, so I'll get some rest. Promise." It wasn't a total lie. He had been taking some recertification with the Texas Commission on Fire Prevention as part of his fire investigator certification.

"Alright. If there's anything you need, I'm here. Got it?"

"Yep. Now, go back to work. I'll have Sally Anne bring you some coffee, you grouch." He smiled at his brother's "jerk" comment, and strode toward the front. After a couple minutes of chatting with Sally Anne, he headed for home.

Beth stared at the large courier envelope she'd tossed onto the middle of her bed. Her neighbors in North Carolina, the Findlay's, had collected her mail for the last few weeks and forwarded everything to her. The growing knot in her stomach seemed to twist and turn, churning inside like a rattlesnake. She knew what the envelope contained. Bills. Letters from collection agencies trying to scare her into sending them money. Money she didn't have. More people trying to squeeze money from a stone, because she didn't have a clue how she was going to pay them.

"Evan, I swear if you weren't already in jail, I'd strangle you with my bare hands. How could you do this to me and Jamie?"

She flopped down onto the bed, and pulled her knees up to her chest. After the whole disaster with her now ex-husband and the Crowley County bond, both she and Tessa had donated all the bond money back to the county. What once had been a prized family possession became tainted and twisted in her duplicitous ex's hands. He'd turned something honorable and historic into nothing more than blood money, and Tessa had agreed when Beth suggested donating it back to the county. Who would have thought her ex-husband would figure out the bond was worth millions of dollars, and hatch an insane plan to kill Tessa and then her?

If he'd succeeded with his maniacal scheme, all the money would have gone to Beth's daughter, Jamie. Evan, as her father, would have gained full control of all that money, and he'd planned to play the poor, widowed father to the hilt.

Weeks after obtaining a divorce, and all the paperwork signed and filed with the court system, Beth found out the true duplicity of her ex-husband's deceit. Bills began showing up, tons of them, addressed to Evan and mailed to her parents' old address. Statements for credit cards she'd never seen. Ones he'd opened by forging her signature. The two additional mortgages on their home—the one they'd bought together in the early days of their marriage—those had been a total shock. She'd only found out about the mortgages when she'd tried to put the house on the market, after she and Jamie had relocated to Shiloh Springs.

That hadn't been the end of his nasty tricks, though. He'd also taken out life insurance policies on Beth and Jamie, worth over two million dollars. And he'd made darn sure he'd kept up the payments on those policies.

She shifted to sit with her legs crossed, and placed the envelope on her lap, closed her eyes and took a deep breath.

Treat it like ripping off a Band-Aid. Yank the sucker off and get it over with, because it's not going away, no matter how hard you ignore it.

She pulled the cardboard zipper and opened the package, upending it and pouring out the contents. They spilled across her lap, the pile getting bigger and bigger. Envelopes with final notice in big red letters, or past due stamps, tumbled out. How could there be so many? How could she have been so blind? Like a gullible fool, she'd believed all his lies. All his sweet promises. Never again. She'd been a naïve idiot, believing a smooth-talking con artist who'd offered words of love and commitment. Now, what remained of her dreams of happily ever after lay in a pile of past due bills and threats of foreclosure.

"Mommy? Why're you crying?"

Beth wiped at her eyes, feeling the wetness against her fingertips. She hadn't even realized she was crying, lost so deep in her thoughts. Worse, she hadn't noticed her precious baby girl come into the room. Jamie was the one good thing Evan had ever given her, and she'd do it all again if it meant she'd have her sweet baby girl.

"Everything's okay, sweetie. Mommy was thinking about something sad, but it's gone now." She pasted on a smile, and patted the bed beside her. "Wanna come up here and snuggle with me?"

Jamie raced across the room, her blonde curls floating behind her, and raised her arms up when she reached the edge of the mattress. Leaning toward her, Beth lifted her daughter onto the bed, and snuggled her against her side, inhaling the scent of her daughter's baby shampoo. She kept her arms wrapped around her daughter, thankful Jamie was too little to understand what her father had done. Sometimes she'd ask about her daddy, and Beth explained he was out of town, and wouldn't be home for a long time. She knew eventually she'd have to tell Jamie the truth, but that was a long time from the here and now. Today, she simply held her daughter close, and wished she could press pause, and keep the rest of the world at bay.

"Can we have faffles for breakfast?"

"You want waffles, huh? Sounds good to me, kiddo. Let's go."

Beth scooted off the bed, picking up Jamie and swirling around with her, holding her up high. She smiled as Jamie giggled, reaching her arms up toward the ceiling.

"Higher, Mommy! Higher!"

"I can't lift you higher, baby girl. You're getting too big. Pretty soon, you're going to have to lift me up instead."

Her words caused Jamie to laugh even more. "I can't pick you up, Mommy. You're a grow'd up. You're too big."

"I'm too big? I'm not too big to tickle you, you little monster!"

Jamie screeched and wrestled playfully in her arms, and Beth let her go, chuckling as Jamie headed toward the kitchen. Time to make her breakfast. She'd developed a fascination with frozen waffles, and wanted them for breakfast, lunch, and dinner. While they were time savers,

Beth didn't want them to be the only thing her daughter ate. But today, she didn't have the heart to say no.

A knock at the front door had her detouring in that direction, Jamie on her heels. Looking through the peep hole in the apartment's door, she spotted Tessa on the other side.

"Morning." She quickly moved out of the way as Jamie barreled toward her aunt.

"Aunt Tessa! Aunt Tessa! We are having faffles! You want some?" Jamie wrapped herself around Tessa's legs, her little arms barely reaching all the way around. "Mommy makes good faffles."

"Faffles?"

"Waffles," Beth motioned toward the kitchen. "Frozen toaster waffles. Jamie has become addicted to them."

"Ah, gotcha." Tessa reached down and smoothed a hand over Jamie's head. "I would love some waffles, but I already ate breakfast. I'll sit with you while you eat yours, though."

Jamie took Tessa's hand and led her into the apartment's miniscule kitchen, Beth trailing behind. She'd rented the place after her last trip to Shiloh Springs, thinking after she sold the house, she'd have enough money to get a better place, maybe even buy a home here. With the disaster Evan had made of her financial life, not only was she in debt up to her eyeballs, her credit was ruined. Tessa didn't know yet, and she wasn't sure how much longer she could expect Serena and Ms. Patti to keep her financial woes a secret. Ms. Patti was the sweetest, kindest woman she'd met in this town, but she was also Tessa's future mother-in-law, which put Beth in a precarious situation. Time to bite the bullet and tell her sister the truth—she was dead broke and drowning in debts she'd had no hand in creating. But, according to the divorce decree, because these debts hadn't been disclosed at the time of the settlement, and all the debt was in both hers and Evan's names, she was responsible for any debt incurred during their marriage. She'd have to go to court, and get a ruling to change that, which she fully intended to do, but the court date was months away. In the meantime, she had a tiny nest egg of savings, one she was using to put a roof over Jamie's head.

"How's everything?"

"We're doing okay." Beth watched Jamie open the freezer drawer and pull out the package of frozen waffles. Her little girl grew more independent with each passing day. With the move from North Carolina to Texas, Beth had pulled her out of pre-kindergarten. She needed to get her enrolled in class in Shiloh Springs, because she didn't want Jamie falling behind all the other kids.

Tessa glanced toward Jamie. "Is you know who still bothering you?"

Beth shook her head. "I haven't heard from him in several weeks. Hopefully he got the message, because I've got nothing to say to him. Can you believe he wants me to come visit him in prison?"

"He's got some nerve. Pleading to lesser charges was the

smartest thing he could've done. Jamie doesn't need to know what her father intended for us."

"The last time he called, he wanted me to bring her to visit him." Beth pulled butter and syrup from the refrigerator, and pulled the toaster to the edge of the counter. Jamie carried her footstool over and climbed up. With the ease of familiarity, she put one waffle and then a second into the slots and pushed down on the button of the toaster.

"Unbelievable."

"What's unbelievable, Aunt Tessa?"

Tessa knelt down until she was eye level with Jamie. "It's unbelievable you are such a big girl, you're making your own breakfast."

"Course I make breakfast. I'm four years old."

"Well, can you stop growing for a little while?"

Jamie giggled. "That's silly."

Tessa glanced at Beth. "Can I ask her?"

Beth nodded. "Sure."

The waffles popped up, and Beth placed them on Jamie's plastic yellow plate. It was her favorite. She quickly added the butter and syrup, and cut the waffles into bite-size pieces before placing the plate on the table, and poured a glass of apple juice for her daughter.

Beth watched Tessa slide onto the seat across from Jamie at the battle-scarred table that came with the furnished apartment. None of it was things she'd pick, but under the circumstances, it'd do until she could figure out her next move.

"Jamie, I've got an important question I want to ask you."

Jamie put down her fork, and folded her hands in her lap. She looked so cute and serious, Beth wanted to grab her phone and snap a picture. But this was Tessa's moment, and she didn't want to spoil the mood.

"Okay, Aunt Tessa."

"You know Uncle Rafe and I are getting married, right?" Jamie's hair bobbed around her shoulders at her vigorous nod.

"I like Uncle Rafe. He's funny."

"Uncle Rafe likes you too, sweetheart. We want to ask if you'll be the flower girl in our wedding. Being a flower girl is a very important job. Maybe one of the most important ones in the whole wedding."

Jaime's forehead scrunched in concern, looking so serious Beth had to hide her smile. "What does a flower girl do?"

"You have to walk down the long row in the church, all the way from the back to the front. You get to wear a pretty new dress, carry a basket of flower petals, and you throw the flowers on the ground while you walk to the front of the church. You come out before the bride—me—so everybody will see how beautiful you look. Do you think you could do that?"

Jamie looked at her mother. "Do you think I can, Mommy?"

"I think you will be a wonderful flower girl, baby." Beth's heart swelled, the pride in her daughter almost overwhelming her. She was growing up so fast, too fast sometimes. While she'd love to freeze time and keep her exactly like she was at this moment, she knew Jamie was going to be an amazing person in her own right someday, and she couldn't wait to see what she'd accomplish.

"Alright, Aunt Tessa, I can be your flower girl." Jamie tapped her finger on the table. "Do I have to grow the flowers? I don't know how."

"No, we'll get you all the flowers you need. Rafe and I are happy to have you be a part of our wedding. Now, come give me a hug, because I'm supposed to meet Ms. Patti to discuss wedding details."

Jamie raced around the table, throwing her arms around Tessa's neck. Beth wrapped her arms across her middle, so proud of her girl.

"I need to talk to your mommy for a minute. Go ahead and finish your waffles." Tessa stood and motioned toward the door. Beth followed her, wondering what Tessa needed to say.

"Ms. Patti and I were talking, and we think you should consider renting the cottage where I'm staying. She's already talked to Old Man Johnson, he's the owner, and he doesn't have any problem with changing the lease over to your name. I'm going to move to the Big House anyway, so Ms. Patti and I have more time to plan the wedding. You won't have to come up with a security deposit or first and last months' rent either. Simply take over my lease and move in."

"Tessa, I don't—"

"Don't even start with me, Sis. You don't need to be living in this apartment, where there's barely enough room for you to turn around. There're two bedrooms in the cottage. It's furnished. Easy enough to turn the second bedroom from an office back into a bedroom. It'll give me peace of mind, and give you time to look around and find a place you really like. Once Rafe and I are married, I'll be moving into his house, which is right down the street. We'll be neighbors. Please, do this. Not just for me, but for Jamie."

"I don't know what to say. Thank you."

"You're doing me a favor. I didn't want to break my lease or have the place sitting empty. It's a win-win."

Beth hugged Tessa tight. "Thank you. And tell Ms. Patti thanks from me."

Tessa laughed. "I swear, she's got her pulse on everything happening in Shiloh Springs. Sometimes I'd swear she's psychic. She'd already talked with Mr. Johnson and made all the arrangements before I even broached the subject. Honestly, all I had to do was ask you to move in."

"Well, I'm grateful, and I know Jamie already loves it."

"Then it's settled. Get your stuff packed, and I'll have Rafe and a couple of the Boudreaus move it over to the cottage."

"What, today?" Beth stared at her sister.

"Why wait? You don't have that much stuff. Shouldn't take them long."

With another hug, Tessa left, and Beth leaned against the closed door. The rent on the cottage wasn't much more than what she was paying for this postage stamp-sized apartment, and would mean a better space for Jamie. Maybe, just maybe, things were looking up.

Smiling, she headed into the kitchen to help her daughter finish breakfast, and start packing their few belongings.

For the first time in months, Beth felt lighter, as if the giant boulder weighing her down had been tossed aside. Evan might have colored her past, mired her in a pit of quicksand financially and emotionally, but she finally felt like she was moving forward again. Moving to Texas to be near Tessa had been the right decision, she knew it in her gut. Fingers crossed, Shiloh Springs would be a new beginning for her and Jamie.

"Come on, kiddo. We've got some packing to do."

CHAPTER TWO

After tossing and turning for a hour, any thoughts of actual sleep disappeared. Brody headed to the kitchen, and reached for the coffee pot, pouring a cup. Strong and black, the way he liked it. Standing in the open back doorway, he stared out at the sweeping panorama of the Boudreau ranch. He loved the old place, felt the connection deep in his soul, and if circumstances were different, he'd probably choose to live here permanently. He could've worked with the horses and the cattle and been happy. But he was compelled, maybe even obsessed, to work with fire. Saving people, saving buildings, it was a calling he couldn't ignore.

Finishing his coffee, he spotted his father walking toward the barn, his stride purposeful, his ever-present cowboy hat pulled low over his brow. The sight evoked a memory from early days, when he'd first come to live at the Big House. While Douglas owned and ran a large and extremely successful construction company, he was as much a part of the working ranch as the dirt beneath his boots. He'd lost count of the times he'd seen the man working alongside the ranch hands, setting posts and mending fences, doing his fair share to keep their homestead running.

Douglas Boudreau held a special place in Brody's heart, had from the day he'd met him. Bigger than life, tall and strong, to a small eight-year-old boy the mountain of a man engendered an imposing and intimidating sight, yet he'd quickly learned Douglas was one of the gentlest men Brody ever met. With a heart as big as Texas, Douglas and Ms. Patti welcomed him into their home and into their hearts, with an ease he found remarkable to this day. He couldn't put into words the special place in his heart these two remarkable people held, helping him bridge the painful gap of heartbreak and loss at a tender age. Some days he could feel Ms. Patti's loving arms wrapped around him while he'd mourned, sharing his grief, his young mind unable to accept the devastating loss and changes, the yawning despair threatening to swallow him whole.

Shaking his head, he rinsed his cup, put it in the dishwasher, and headed out to the barn. Maybe a little strenuous exercise might help clear his head, make sense of the jumbled thoughts rolling around inside his brain.

While he'd tried in vain to sleep, all he'd thought about, fantasized about, was Beth Stewart. Beautiful, headstrong, and independent, she'd moved halfway across the country to make a clean break with painful memories and a messy divorce. She was making a new life for her and her daughter in a new town under strained and stressful circumstances.

Though she'd been welcomed as part of the Boudreau family, he didn't feel anything close to familial about the feisty woman who kept him fantasizing about a future which could never be.

When Brody walked into the barn, Douglas sat atop a wooden stool holding a bridle, studying it with the same intensity he did everything else. The worn leather looked tiny within his father's big, work-roughened hands. His dad looked up when Brody walked in, his face a study of lines and angles, tanned from working outdoors his entire life. Years in the military as an Army Ranger trained and disciplined him into a strong man, one with a compassionate heart and an easy smile. Hands toughened and scarred from construction work, as well as daily life on the ranch, their touch could yield a gentleness belied by his size, or a swat to a backside when deserved.

"Morning, son. Heard you had a tough night."

"That it was, Dad. Blaze at the Summers' place. A bad one. Thankfully, we caught it in time before it spread too far."

"It's a shame, place lying abandoned. It's a good piece of property. Any idea what caused it?"

Brody hesitated, not wanting to make any unfounded assumptions, but his father knew the lay of the land when it came to things happening in and around Shiloh Springs. He'd spent most of his adult life here after leaving the military, and was well respected by everyone in their small community. He also had a good head on his shoulders when it came to people. Soft spoken and not given to saying much, when he did offer his opinion, people listened. Douglas sometimes reminded him of a throwback to a different time, when a man's word meant something. His father was a fair man, one who he trusted implicitly, and knew whatever he told Douglas would be kept between them.

"I don't have any proof yet, but I think the fire was deliberately set."

His father stiffened slightly, before turning his attention back to the bridle. "You're thinking arson?"

"The burn pattern outside the barn indicated that possibility. I'll know more once I can investigate further. I hope I'm wrong, but my gut says otherwise. What I can't figure out is why. There's no motive. The place is abandoned, has been for ages. The Summers have had it on the market forever. Who'd want to torch the old barn?"

Douglas laid the bridle down on the ground by his feet and stood. "Ben Summers wants to sell the place, but he's asking too much. Your momma hasn't been able to convince the family they're overpriced. Sometimes sentimental attachments color people's judgment. Don't know if they're hurting for money. I do know it was a hard decision when Sandra took sick, and the doctors told him she needed to be in a warmer climate. Living in Florida ain't cheap."

"Part of the investigation will be looking at the owners. It's routine. With any insurance payout, it almost always focuses on whether or not arson is suspected."

"I don't think Ben's carried insurance on the place for the last couple of years, son. Doubt it, to be honest. Last he told me, if he wasn't gonna live there, he wasn't concerned about it falling down. Their son doesn't want it. He lives in San Antonio and couldn't care less about running a farm, which is why Ben put it on the market in the first place. Doubt they'll ever come back to Shiloh Springs."

"It's a real shame, because with some hard work and a little money, it could be a beautiful farm again. The barn's gone now, but the house was far enough away there wasn't any damage. I imagine for the right price, it would be snatched up in a heartbeat."

"Your momma's gotten more than a few nibbles, but Ben's hardheaded, and doesn't want to give the place away for a penny less than what he thinks it's worth. Stubborn old goat."

Brody sighed before moving to stand beside his father. He reached out and scratched Tootsie behind the ear. Tootsie had been around almost as long as he'd been living on the ranch, and though she couldn't do much heavy labor anymore, she was spoiled rotten by all the Boudreaus. She butted her head against his hand when he stopped scratching, and he resumed again with a chuckle. Yep, spoiled rotten.

"Something else bothering you, son?" His father leaned against the stall door, his back against the worn wood, ankles crossed, completely relaxed and in his element.

"Nothing. I mean—it's not important."

Douglas straightened to his full height, and caught Brody's shoulders in his strong grip. "You know you can tell me anything, and it stays right here, between us. If it's important to you, then it's important to me. You can talk to me about anything."

The tightness in his chest nearly choked him, the emotional support from the man he admired most in the world threatening to bring him to his knees. His father had been a bulwark in his childhood, an example of how a man should live and treat those around him throughout Brody's teen years, the perfect example of a man who wasn't afraid to love a woman with all his heart, and not be ashamed or embarrassed about who he was or the choices he made as an adult. If anybody would understand his dilemma, it was Douglas Boudreau.

"I've got a problem, Dad."

"Want to tell me about it?"

Brody nodded. "I think I'm falling for Beth Stewart. I know it's wrong, but—"

"Why's it wrong?" His father seemed genuinely surprised at Brody's admission.

"She's Tessa's sister. Tessa, the woman who's engaged to Rafe. The woman who's soon going to be my sister-in-law."

"And?"

"What do you mean 'and'? Beth is going to be part of

this family through her sister. What happens if things don't work out between us? I can't do that to Rafe or Tessa. Tessa and Beth are sisters, close ones. I don't want to cause a problem, do anything that might drive a wedge between them, or worse between Beth and Rafe."

Douglas studied him with an intensity Brody felt all the way to his bones, his stare not judgmental or condemning, but tinged with compassion and understanding. A tiny glimmer of hope started growing deep inside.

"I think you're looking at this all wrong, son. Rafe and Tessa love each other and they're deliriously happy. They're getting married soon, and your wanting to date Tessa's sister isn't going to stop their nuptials. The only person who might have a problem with you dating Beth is—Beth. She's been through the wringer over this whole episode with her ex-husband. It can't have been easy having her life thrown into turmoil."

"I know. Thinking about what she's been through is another reason I've kept my distance."

Douglas leaned back against the stall, once again relaxed and at ease. "Beth strikes me as a strong woman. Independent and sensible. She has to be, raising her daughter on her own."

Brody smiled thinking about Beth's little girl. "She's doing an amazing job with Jamie."

"You'll get no argument from me. She's a precious mite. Plus Jamie loves you, so that's not an issue."

Brody ran his hand along his jawline, scratching at the stubble. He'd grabbed a shower before falling into bed, but hadn't bothered to shave. Another thing he had to take care of before heading back into town.

"I don't want to make a mistake. It'd be different if I only had to worry about me getting hurt. But there are too many people whose lives could be affected if I screw things up."

"Son, take a seat. I'm gonna tell you something I haven't talked about since I was about your age."

Brody slid down to sit on the barn's floor, and leaned back against the wall. The look on his father's face, the seriousness reflected in his expression, told Brody more than words whatever his dad wanted to talk about wasn't something he shared lightly.

"You know I was in the Army."

"The Rangers. Momma's got your medals in that shadowbox above the mantle in the parlor."

"I was stationed overseas a year after I enlisted. This was before I met your momma. Anyway, I came back to the States on leave, and decided to spend some time with my brother."

"Which one?"

"Etienne—your Uncle Gator. He'd moved to New Orleans by then. Left the military, and was doing some contract work."

At his father's pause, Brody nodded. He'd heard stories

about his uncle's extracurricular activities after he came back from Vietnam, though there were some folks who said he'd started working behind the scenes while still enlisted and serving in 'Nam. It was all very hush-hush, and nobody had ever been able to prove exactly what Gator Boudreau did or didn't do. He'd simply disappear for days or weeks at a time, and then show back up to his wife and family.

"I was a brash youngster back then. I worked hard and I played hard. I also made one of the biggest mistakes of my life. I was twenty years old, and raring to have as much fun as I could cram into a few weeks' leave. I spent days with your uncle out in the bayou, fishing and drinking. Then one day, he simply wasn't there. Left me a note, said he'd try and get back before I had to ship out back to Germany, and that was it."

Brody watched his father pick up the bridle he'd been repairing earlier, and start smoothing over the leather, as if he needed something in his hands to anchor him. It didn't seem like a nervous action; it was more like it comforted him to have something substantial in his hands.

"I headed into New Orleans, determined to spend what time I had left with a pretty girl and all the excitement I could dig up in the city. That's where I met Elizabeth."

Brody started at the name. He recognized it, though he'd never been fortunate enough to meet the woman in person. The knot in the pit of his stomach grew, because he had a feeling he knew where his father's story was heading.

"Dad—"

"Elizabeth was everything I was looking for. Beautiful, compassionate, headstrong. Ready to have fun in the French Quarter. We both knew we wouldn't have a lot of time together. I was upfront from the start I had to head back to Germany. She had plans to start college classes at the beginning of the semester. The time I spent with Elizabeth became the highlight of my trip, and I found myself falling for her. Head over heels. I thought she felt the same, and I think she did—until she laid eyes on Gator."

Well, crap.

"I never stood a chance. It wasn't anybody's fault. Gator didn't come back to New Orleans thinking he was going to meet the girl of his dreams. Elizabeth didn't set out to hurt me, either. I won't say it didn't sting my heart, but I think it was more a slap to my pride. I found the girl first; I should have won her heart. But sometimes it's not meant to be. Elizabeth and Gator? They *were* meant to be. Their attraction was palpable, so strong you could almost see their hearts beating as one. I know it sounds all girly and romantic and stuff, but doesn't change the fact it happened. I could have let it drive a wedge between me and my brother. Instead, I got to see a man I admire more than anyone find the happiness he deserved, with a woman who loved him until the day she died."

"So you think Rafe will understand how I feel about Beth?"

Douglas nodded. "He probably already knows how you feel. I hate to break it to you, son, but I doubt there's anybody in this family who doesn't know you've got feelings for Beth. If it concerns you, talk to your brother. Let him know how you feel. Yeah, I know it's not manly to talk about feelings. Don't let stupid stereotypes and fools make you believe for one second your feelings, your emotions, don't count. That's a sure path to unhappiness."

"Thanks, Dad." Brody stood up and brushed the loose pieces of hay off his jeans. "I have to ask. Things between you and Uncle Gator, did they change after he met Elizabeth?"

Douglas shrugged, and walked beside Brody toward the open barn door. "At first there was some awkwardness. I had to go back to Germany. Gator stuck around New Orleans. A couple of weeks after I left, I got a call from him. He and Elizabeth got married in a quiet little ceremony. I was the first person they called, because they didn't want them being together to keep me and my brother apart. Gotta admit, I was hurt. Said some things I wished I could take back the moment they left my mouth, but I was a stubborn fool, and shoved my foot so far down my throat, I figured there was no turning back from it. Took me a couple of weeks to figure out it wasn't my heart getting broke that bothered me. It was my pride. Once I came to terms with being a big, fat jerk, I wrote to Gator and Elizabeth, let them know I regretted how I'd reacted, and I was sorry for the things I'd said."

"They forgave you?"

Douglas chuckled. "They named their son after me. Jean-Luc Douglas Boudreau. When he went into the service, he got the nickname 'Ranger' after me too. We made things right, me and Gator, by not being stubborn and letting our pride blind us to the fact we're family."

Brody hugged his father, feeling his dad's arms wrap around him, enveloping him in the warmth of family he'd felt from the day he'd moved in with Douglas. As usual, his father was right, which was why he'd come to him for advice. He'd talk to Rafe, let him know about his feelings for Beth.

"Thanks, Dad. For everything."

"Any time, Brody. I'm always here for you. Always."

He headed back toward the house, a lightness inside that had been missing for far too long. Things were finally looking up.

CHAPTER THREE

J amie raced through the front door of the cottage, her trilling laughter filling the air. Beth stood behind on the front porch and watched her daughter spin in circles on the hardwood floor, her excitement matching Jamie's, but she reined it in, knowing she had to keep Jamie calm during the move. The rest of the Boudreau clan would be along any minute with the remainder of her things, and she needed that time to simply breathe. Though she loved Shiloh Springs, the whole ordeal with Evan, the move, and then finding out she was broker than broke—well, that tended to put a damper on everything. But she wasn't about to spoil Jamie's excitement. Maybe some of her infectious enthusiasm would rub off.

"Sweetheart, what do you think of the new place?"

"Mommy," Jamie raced up and flung her arms around her mother's waist, "do we really get to live here?"

"Yes, honey, we really get to live here. Your Aunt Tessa is going to live at the Boudreau house with Douglas and Ms. Patti until she marries Uncle Rafe, and she's going to let us stay here. Isn't that great?"

"Yay! Yay! Yay!" Beth was pretty sure Jamie's excited shouts could be heard down the entire block, but before she could shush her, the sound of a car pulling into the drive had her spinning around, her heartbeat ticking up. Brody's pickup stopped behind her small sedan, dwarfing it on the gravel driveway. She crossed her arms over her chest, and drew in a deep breath. Something about Brody Boudreau pulled to her in a way she hadn't felt in a long time. Maybe ever. She shoved the feeling down deep, unwilling to even entertain the thought of exploring any attraction to Brody. The ink was barely dry on her divorce decree, because Evan had fought tooth and nail to keep the divorce from happening, even from behind bars. She'd yet to figure out why he'd fought so hard to stay married, because the idiot had to realize once she knew the truth about his despicable actions, there wasn't a chance in hades she'd stay married to him. He'd planned to kill her. Murder her for money. A chill raced down her spine at the thought. How could she have been so wrong about the man she thought she loved?

Giving a mental shake, she started down the steps, headed for Brody's truck. She watched his tall frame unfold from the driver's seat, and her breath caught at the sight of sunlight glinting off his sandy-brown hair before he placed his black Stetson atop his head. His quick grin caused a fluttering in her stomach, and she placed her hand against it, silently willing the feeling to go away.

Not going there, nu-uh. Brody Boudreau is off the menu, no matter how delicious he looks.

"Uncle Brody!" A whirling dervish of skinny legs and flying ponytails raced past Beth, and dove straight at Brody. Her daughter's giggles increased when Brody swung her up in the air and caught her, spinning her around. The breath caught in her throat with the realization Jamie's father had never done that with their little girl. Then again, there were a lot of things Evan had never done. In hindsight, the marriage she'd thought picture perfect turned out to be little more than paper posies, easily tossed aside when the lure of something new and shiny came along.

"Hey, honey bear." Brody's deep voice yanked Beth back to the present. "Think you can carry this box for me?" He pointed to one of the biggest boxes in the back of his truck.

Jamie laughed again. "Uncle Brody, that one's too big. Mommy can carry it. Give me a littler one."

"You sure? Let me see your muscles." He made a big show of examining her arm when Jamie flexed. "Well, you seem pretty strong, but let's give you one a little bit smaller." Her daughter held her arms up and Brody handed her a much smaller box, one holding kitchen towels and pot holders.

"Be careful, sweetheart," Beth called out.

"I've got it, Mommy." Jamie took deliberately slow steps up to the porch and then turned to look at her. "Where should I put this box, Mommy?"

"That one goes in the kitchen, baby."

Beth drew in a deep breath, watching her little girl head through the front door with her precious cargo. Jaime had been through so much in the last months, being uprooted from the only home she'd known, and then losing her father. She was handling things better than anybody could ask. Jamie never complained, always had a smile for everyone. One day she knew she'd have to explain why her daddy wasn't around anymore, but right now she was too little to understand. And really, what could she say? Tell her daughter her daddy was a monster and needed to be locked in a cell to keep her safe?

Brody strode past her, arms stacked with boxes, and she noticed the way his muscles moved and flexed beneath his navy blue T-shirt. He moved with the confidence of a man comfortable with himself and the world around him, and she only wished she had a smidgen of his calm demeanor. Instead, she felt like the biggest fraud, because nothing in her world felt right. Everything seemed off-kilter. She didn't even fit in the skin she wore like armor, keeping away the ills of the world. If she was honest, it had been like that for longer than she cared to admit. Even before Evan started acting elusive, she'd felt uneasy, off balance. Now, after the revelations of her ex-husband's duplicity, her self-esteem and confidence in herself as a wife, mother, even as a woman, had been chiseled away until she felt like a hollow shell.

Brody walked past her and back down the porch steps, with Jaime trailing behind him like a shadow. Beth forced her feet to take one step and then another, following them to Brody's truck. Reaching into the back, she pulled one of the remaining boxes forward and headed for the house. There really weren't that many. Most of their belongings were still in North Carolina, in a locked storage unit she paid for monthly. Straightening her spine, she carried the box into the master bedroom and set it on the end of the bed.

Turning toward the door, she gasped when she spotted Brody in the open doorway, two boxes stacked in his arms.

"Sorry, didn't mean to startle you. Where do you want these?" He nodded toward the unlabeled boxes.

She pointed toward the floor inside the bedroom. "Just put them there by the door."

"No problem." He flashed a smile as he followed her instructions. "Only a couple more to go."

"Thank you. I appreciate you helping me...us get settled."

"That's what family's for, Beth. You're Tessa's family, and by extension that makes you part of the Boudreau clan." He winked before heading down the hall, and Beth felt that ever-present-around-Brody-Boudreau fluttery sensation in her stomach again. There was something about Brody that made her blood sing.

"Stop it," she muttered, dispelling the spell he seemed to put her under. It was too little, too late. She wasn't ever falling into the relationship trap again. Been there, done that, and wouldn't wear the lousy T-shirt on a bet.

Voices from the front of the cottage drew her attention toward the door, and she spotted Rafe and Tessa, along with Douglas and Ms. Patti, standing on the front porch. Tessa grinned and waved, and Beth motioned for her to come in. Ms. Patti and Tessa walked into the living room, while Rafe and Douglas headed back down the steps of the front porch toward their cars.

"Brody mentioned he's almost finished bringing your stuff in. Ms. Patti and I brought along a few supplies to help stock your fridge, so you don't have to worry about doing grocery shopping for a few days."

"You didn't have to do that, but thank you." Beth's eyes widened as Rafe and Douglas strode past her toward the kitchen, arms loaded with grocery bags. "Guys, that's far too much—"

"Nonsense." Ms. Patti pulled her into a hug, and thumped her on the back. Beth squeaked a little at the bear hug. Ms. Patti was remarkably strong for such a tiny woman. Then again, Beth mused, having raised a passel of boys from youngsters into men, she'd have to be. Tessa grinned at the blonde-haired dynamo, and Beth linked arms with her sister, following her inside. Ms. Patti marched into the kitchen and began giving orders to Rafe and Douglas, who stood in the center of the room, looking lost and confused. She reminded Beth of a drill sergeant, her no-nonsense attitude getting the job done, her will indomitable even facing down two men bigger than her by nearly a foot.

Out of the corner of her eye, she watched Brody place a couple more boxes against the wall in the living room. His lips quirked up in a grin as he watched his mother ordering around the others, softly chuckling when they hurried to fulfill her every request.

"She's really something, isn't she?" Tessa's words were whispered, and Beth nodded. "This is nothing. You should see her with the wedding plans. She's got people jumping, bending over backward, ready to accomplish whatever she wants. People in Shiloh Springs practically worship the ground she walks on. Honestly, I don't think I could do half of what she's done in such a short time." Tessa leaned in and added conspiratorially, "I want to be just like her when I grow up." Her words were accompanied with a cheeky grin.

"Brody," Ms. Patti glanced toward her son, "if you're done moving boxes, could you please grab the hamper on the back seat of my car?"

"Yes, ma'am."

Ms. Patti watched her son walk out the front door before smiling at Beth. "He's a good son, and an equally good man." She rubbed her hands together, the spark in her eyes matched by her satisfied grin. "I brought two pans of lasagna, a couple loaves of garlic bread, and salad fixings. Oh, and there's a gallon of sweet tea, and a gallon of lemonade on the back floor of my car."

"I'll help Brody bring it in, Momma." Rafe dropped a kiss on his mother's cheek as he walked past her.

"I got a good one, too." Tessa leaned her chin on Beth's shoulder. "I promise, Sis, everything will work out. Wait and see."

"I hope you're right."

"Mommy, did you see? They bringed us, I mean brought us, two boxes of faffles. I get faffles for breakfast!" Jamie held up the frozen breakfast treats like they were trophies she'd won, waving the brightly packaged boxes over her head.

Beth burst out laughing. "I swear, Jaime, you eat too many of them and you're going to turn into a waffle. There are other things to have for breakfast, you know."

"Let the child have her waffles. Having a healthy appetite is a good thing, especially at her age." Ms. Patti pulled Jaime against her side, and ruffled her hair. "Personally, I love frozen waffles in the morning."

"Since when?" Beth heard the softly muttered question from Douglas as he closed the freezer door. She bit her lip to keep for laughing. Being around the Boudreaus made her smile and forget about her troubles, at least for a little while. Plus, seeing her sister in love and happy helped make everything better too.

Brody and Rafe trooped into the kitchen, their arms loaded down with the food and drinks Ms. Patti brought. Beth raced over to the cupboard, hand raised to open it, before realizing the few dishes she had were packed in the boxes stacked along the kitchen wall. Her sister walked over and opened the cupboard Beth had reached for, revealing stacks of plates, bowls, and glasses, all neatly arranged exactly how she'd have done it.

"I left my stuff here. You and Jamie can use them, since I've already got brand new ones as wedding gifts. One less thing you need to worry about. Besides, once you get your stuff out of storage in North Carolina and shipped down here, you'll have more than enough."

Beth bit her lower lip to keep from crying, overwhelmed at her sister's generosity. She felt like the biggest fraud, because she still hadn't mentioned to Tessa about the nightmare she faced dealing with the fallout of her ex's mountain of debt. Even paying the tab on the storage unit in North Carolina ate into her small nest egg, which wouldn't last much longer unless she got a job. Or won the lottery.

Tessa pulled a stack of plates down and handed them to Rafe, with a quick kiss on his cheek. She quickly grabbed glasses and started filling them with ice, while Ms. Patti and Tessa started serving up the impromptu lunch. Passing around the glasses, she filled them with sweet tea and lemonade. The lasagna was still warm, the salad crisp and the perfect accompaniment.

Once all the plates were filled, everyone moved to the living room, since there weren't enough seats at the kitchen table, which only sat four. Beth balanced her plate on her knee, and watched everyone dig into their food, smiling at the feeling of family surrounding her. It was moments like this when she missed her parents. Family dinners had been a big thing in her home growing up. Even after she moved out for college, she managed to get home at least once or twice a week, loving catching up on the little things.

Those family dinners had dwindled over time once she'd married Evan. He'd never come right out and said he didn't want to go, but somehow, he'd always have something else planned for them on the same day. His feigned interest made her enjoyment of being around her family strained. Knew her mother and father felt it too, though they never uttered a word.

But sitting here, in the center of another family, that feeling of warmth, of belonging, sparked deep within. She wanted Jamie to know what it meant to be part of something bigger, to know other people cared for her, the way Beth's family had loved Beth and Tessa. Glancing toward her daughter, who sat cross-legged on the floor, her mouth smeared with sauce, Beth felt like she was finally home.

"Momma, this is awesome." Rafe stood and dropped a kiss on the top of his mother's head. "I'm gonna grab another piece."

"Wait for me, bro. I want more too." Brody stood, and his eyes met Beth's. A tingling warmth filled her belly when his stare roved over her, lingering on her mouth. For a brief second, the hunger in his gaze made her think he wanted more than food. She broke eye contact, though it was hard. How could she feel like this?

"Ms. Patti, Douglas, I can't thank you enough. I don't

know what I'd have done without your help."

Ms. Patti reached over and squeezed Beth's hand. "You'd have done fine. We're glad you're here, with your family."

"You need anything, you call me. Or Ms. Patti." Douglas' gruff voice, deep and rumbly, was belied by the twinkle in his eyes. He was a big man, well over six feet, and muscled from his years of construction work. Though he wasn't a big talker, not that she'd noticed anyway, everyone paid attention when he spoke.

"I will, I promise."

Once everyone had eaten their fill, the leftovers were packed up and put in the refrigerator. Beth was surprised they'd gone through an entire tray of lasagna and part of the second one. She chuckled. Those Boudreau men sure could pack away a lot of food.

Walking to the door, she waved as their vehicles drove away, leaving her and Jamie to settle into their new home. Heading back inside, she ran her hand over the back of a chair, taking in the cozy living room. Tessa had told her about the break-in, how everything had been ransacked and destroyed, including the furniture that came with the rented house.

Her hand tightened on the back of the chair. This furniture, all of it, belonged to Brody. All of it had been in storage, and he'd immediately offered it to Tessa, to replace the stuff that had been unsalvageable. Taking in the warm butterscotch tones of the leather sofa and matching chairs, she had to admit he had good taste. Her sister had added a few simple touches, pops of color, making the house feel like a home.

A home Beth now shared with her baby girl. A noise behind her had her spinning around, catching her daughter with a cookie halfway to her mouth. Beth raised her brow, and nodded toward the cookie.

"Where'd that come from, young lady?"

"Ms. Patti gave it to me."

"I don't remember seeing any cookies."

Jamie grinned and pointed to the freezer. "Mr. Douglas put them in the freezer, so they stay fresh. He said there's a whole package just for me."

"Oh, really? So, I don't get any cookies, huh?"

Jamie giggled. "You gotta say please and thank you."

Beth stepped forward and ruffled her daughter's hair. "May I please have a cookie?"

"Yes. Ms. Patti said to cook it in the micro-something to make it taste better."

Beth pointed to the cookie in Jamie's hand. "The microwave, and yes, that makes them all warm and gooey. Want me to heat one up for you?"

"That's okay, I like it this way too. Can I go play?"

"Right after I get a hug. Stay on the porch though."

"Okay, Mommy." Jamie wrapped her arms around Beth's waist and squeezed, then darted through the kitchen and out the front door. Beth watched her for a few minutes through the open door, and knew her baby was safe. Leaning down, she lifted one of the boxes piled against the kitchen wall, set it on the table, and pulled back the tape. Might as well get some things put away.

She was barely halfway through the box when her cell phone rang. Looking at the caller ID, her stomach plummeted. Not again. When would her ex learn? She wasn't coming for a visit to the prison. And she definitely wasn't bringing Jamie to see her father in such a place. Was he insane?

Swiping to disconnect the call, before she could put the phone down it rang again. Only this time, it wasn't Evan.

CHAPTER FOUR

Evan Stewart paced the length of his cell, his footsteps barely making a sound with each step. He couldn't stay still. It felt like a million ants crawled inside his body, giving him the heebie-jeebies. He really couldn't stand being locked up inside this cell. Caged like a stinking animal. It wasn't right. Nothing about this whole fiasco was right.

Add in his ex-wife still wasn't taking his calls. He'd tried again half an hour ago, and she hadn't answered. Did she really think he was going to go away so easily? Fade into the woodwork and let her live a happy little life, while he wasted away behind bars? He growled deep in his throat. She really had another think coming if she believed that scenario.

Never claiming patience as his strong suit, spending one second more in this dank, depressing pit irritated his last nerve. He didn't deserve to be behind bars. The blame rested solely on Trevor's shoulders. How had he allowed the scrawny numbskull to convince him grabbing Tessa was a good idea? He'd been content to play a slow, tortuous game of cat-and-mouse with his sister-in-law, and it had only been a matter of time until he'd have had his hands on the

Crowley County bond and the millions of dollars it represented. Instead, Trevor's obsession with Evan's sister-in-law colored his judgment, believing she'd come rushing back into his arms. Yeah, right. Like that had happened. Not only had Tessa not given them the county bond, she'd involved the stupid sheriff over in Shiloh Springs. He and his brother had cost Evan everything.

If she'd only given me the bond, none of this would've happened.

Another circuit of his cell, hands clenched into fists at his side. He cursed the day he'd met his wife, Beth Maxwell. Like a fool, he'd been infatuated from the start. She'd been the prettiest girl he'd ever seen. The sound of her laughter drew him in, captivated him, until he'd tumbled head over heels. Yeah, they'd been happy—until they weren't.

Never in a million years did he think he'd get tired of Beth. His wife. His lover. The proverbial noose around his neck.

Traveling had been a godsend at first. Business kept him on the road a few times a year. The first time he'd slept with another woman, violated his marriage vows, he'd been eaten up with guilt. Swore it would never happen again. But it did. Over and over. It got easier to volunteer for out-of-town jobs, seminars, anything to leave Beth and North Carolina in his rearview mirror. The excitement of new places, bigger cities, and the draw of illicit hookups seduced him, addicted his mind and his body, until all he thought about was freedom—freedom from his mundane life and the shackles cobbling him to a now loveless marriage.

Then Beth got pregnant.

The shock of her joy-filled announcement hit him like a ton of bricks. He didn't want kids. Never had. Didn't even like being around them, especially other people's children. They were nasty, messy, deplorable things that slowly drained away your will to live. Why'd she have to get pregnant? She'd been on the pill, he knew, because he checked religiously to make sure she didn't miss any. Beth wanted children eventually, but he'd convinced her they should wait until he was better established at his job. They'd have the time and money to dedicate themselves to raising a family then. Not that he ever intended to have any of the stinky little buggers.

Now he had an ex and a brat, and between them they'd managed to ruin everything. If only he'd stuck to his plan, he'd be sitting pretty on Easy Street, a bereaved widower with a small motherless child. Jamie, his daughter, would have inherited her mother's share of the millions, and he'd hire an au pair to take care of the sniveling brat, while he lived the life he deserved. Everything would have been perfect, exactly like he'd pictured in his mind a thousand times. Until Tessa and her sheriff boyfriend ruined all of his perfect plans.

He closed his eyes and drew in a long, slow breath, holding it for a minute before exhaling. Calm, he needed to be calm. He couldn't afford to tip his hand. Not when things were finally falling into place. Patience was the key.

His eyes flew open at the sound of his cell door opening, and his roommate stepped through, his lips twisted in a sardonic smirk. The cold, black deadness of his eyes chilled Evan to the depths of his soul, but he couldn't afford to be squeamish, not with his whole future in the other man's tattoo-covered hands.

Neither spoke until the door was secured and the guard was out of earshot. "Well, how'd it go?"

"Looking good, dude. My cousin and his old lady got everything lined up. Long as we meet up with 'em, they'll make sure we get across the border into Mexico. They know a place to cross without getting caught." The tall African-American man strode past Evan, flung himself down on his bunk, and folded his hands beneath his shaved head. Though he did his best to hide it, the terror inside Evan stank like putrid flop sweat. Compared to Axel, who worked out every day and had muscles a steroid abuser would worship, he felt like a ninety-eight-pound weakling.

"When?"

"Chill, man. It'll happen when it happens. Soon, though. Things are coming together; it won't be long now."

Evan's frustrated growl evidenced his irritation. He hated being at the mercy of others. Look what happened the last time he'd listened to somebody else. Trevor had screwed up. Now he had to trust another, and his gut roiled at the thought. Too many things could go wrong, as he'd learned the hard way. But he had to wait on Axel, because this was his plan and his people.

Getting out from behind these bars, these walls, had become his one priority, his sole focus. Only then could he put in motion his real plan. Axel and his buddies had made it clear: they were heading for the border and crossing into Mexico the minute they escaped from here. Evan had other ideas, and he planned on splintering off from Axel and his crew the first chance he got. While the locals and the feds were chasing after the escapees, Evan planned on being hundreds of miles away, deep in the heart of Texas.

Specifically, Shiloh Springs, Texas. Where his ex-wife and child currently resided, along with his traitorous sister-in-law.

Revenge against Tessa would be sweet, unfortunately, it wouldn't be swift. She was too well-guarded by her boyfriend, the sheriff. No, his plans focused around his ex.

He knew she'd obtained a divorce. His lawyer brought him the papers, and advised him to sign them. Blathered some nonsense about it looking good on his record that he was cooperating in the face of all his charges. He'd signed them. Let them think he was a model prisoner, right up until he slipped through their fingers like a puff of smoke.

"You listening to me, man?" Axel shifted on the narrow cot, leaning against the painted cinderblock wall, his face obscured by shadows from the upper bunk. The deep baritone of his voice matched his muscular frame, the sound menacing and disturbing. Evan felt a bead of sweat trickle down the side of his face. Axel had been behind bars on and off for the better part of his adult life, for a string of bad choices and worst acts. Nobody with half a brain would ever accuse Axel of being a nice guy. They didn't cross him, either. Somehow, and he still wasn't quite sure why, Axel had befriended him almost from the day he'd walked through the cell door into their shared space. Never one to look a gift horse in the mouth, and frankly terrified about spending what could be a good chunk of the rest of his life in Huntsville, Evan latched onto Axel's offer of friendship and protection, never realizing the big black man held the answer to his prayers—getting out of this hellhole.

"I hear you. I'm just sick of these four walls."

Axel shrugged. "You get used to it."

"Never."

"Keep things on the down low, few more days, man. Then it'll be tequila and senoritas, and beaches for miles. No bars on the doors and windows, and especially no cops." Axel let out a contented-sounding sigh. "I ain't never coming back to Texas, man. I'm gonna live the high life down south of the border, you feel me? Little bit of money down there buys a lot of happiness."

"Can't be soon enough for me," Evan muttered, pacing across the narrow space to stare out the small barred window overlooking the yard, staring at the swath of concrete and dirt. He focused his mind on his main objective, repeating it over and over, like a personal mantra.

I'll have my freedom and Beth will pay.

CHAPTER FIVE

The next morning, after having helped Beth move over to Tessa's rental, Brody drove over to the Summers place. He parked several feet from the charred remains of the old Summers' barn, the acrid smell of burned wood still perfuming the air.

Climbing out, he grabbed the kit he kept in the bed of his truck. The one he used when he investigated scenes he felt were suspicious—like this one. This entire scenario screamed setup to him, from the deserted location to the visible trails of superheated scorch marks.

He quickly donned a set of gloves. The less contamination of the scene, the better. Ducking beneath the bright yellow caution tape his crew had used to cordon off the area, he straightened, scanning the ground for evidence. He knew how important it was to take his time, look for any clues. Sometimes the most insignificant things made the difference in determining a fire's triggering incident. Taking each step slow and methodical, he watched where he walked, did a circuit around the remnants of the barn, making a visual note of all his surroundings.

After the fire, he'd gone through the site, documenting the fire's aftereffects with photos and video. Collected and bagged evidence. It had been pitch-black, other than the lights from the firetrucks and headlights from his personal truck, but he'd conducted an initial investigation, knowing every aspect of the scene needed to be carefully and thoroughly documented. But something didn't feel right, so he'd come back this morning to take another look. Possibly gather any evidence that might have been missed or overlooked, to send to the forensic laboratory in Austin.

Unfortunately, the Summers' barn didn't have a whole lot left to identify. The roof had caved in from a combination of the flames and the high velocity of the water used to put out the fire. A couple of structural beams still remained, blackened and scarred from the heat. Large chunks of the walls were gone, debris scattered in darkened husks on the ground inside where the building once stood.

Brody shook his head. He remembered playing in this barn growing up, spending hours with Greg Summers talking about horses, what they wanted to do when they grew up, and girls. Shoot, he'd probably spent as much time with Greg and his family as he had at his house. Douglas and Ms. Patti encouraged Brody to make friends, knowing he needed to be with others outside his brothers at the Big House. It had taken him a while to fit in with the other boys—his brothers—and Greg had been his best friend in Shiloh Springs. Too bad they'd grown apart once Greg moved to San Antonio. He hadn't loved small-town life, not the way Brody did. Greg had hightailed it out of town the first opportunity he got. He'd come around occasionally to visit his folks, but now even those visits had pretty much dried up since his parents moved to South Florida.

A glint of something at his feet caught his eye. He stooped and ran a gloved finger across the piece of glass. Lifting it from the dirt, Brody examined it, noting a small piece of paper, some kind of label maybe, still adhered to the fragment. Pulling a plastic bag from his pocket, he slid the shard inside, sealed and labeled it as evidence. Good thing he'd grabbed a couple of baggies at the same time he'd picked up the gloves. It was hard to tell how long the glass had been there, but sitting on top of the packed earth, it was safe to assume it hadn't been there all that long. If he was lucky, they might be able to get some prints off it. He couldn't help wondering if it had been part of a container used to start the blaze.

He walked the interior of what was left of the charred husk, picking up a few more fragments of bottle and one singed piece of fabric, which smelled suspiciously like gasoline. Might be kerosene, it was hard to tell. Shaking his head, he shoved it into a separate evidence bag, all too sure now his suspicions were correct.

This fire had been no accident. He was dealing with an arsonist. Shiloh Springs had their very own firebug, and he was escalating. Brody decided to do one more sweep of the barn, and then he'd head into town. The evidence he'd collected needed to be sent for gas chromatography and mass spectrometry to help determine what chemical or chemicals were used, though he felt certain they'd find gasoline as the culprit. If they were lucky, they might be able to lift some DNA from the pieces of glass.

Brody straightened and glanced toward the dirt road when he heard a vehicle pull up, and watched Rafe climb out of his pickup and walk toward the yellow caution tape.

"I suspected I'd find you here. Find anything?" Rafe stayed on the other side of the caution tape barrier, which Brody appreciated. The less contamination of the scene the better. It had taken hours to douse the blaze, and by the time they'd contained it, everyone was exhausted. He'd walked the perimeter, looking and studying it for clues. Evidence. Any items which might help him determine what had ignited the barn. Or in this case who—because he was certain this hadn't occurred naturally. It had been helped along by somebody, and that pissed him off.

Brody held up the dozen evidence bags with the items he'd collected. "Found enough to convince me we have a serious problem."

Rafe pushed his cowboy hat back and glared at the baggies, a scowl marring his expression. "You're sure it's arson?"

"As sure as I can be, until I can deliver these for testing. But from the burn pattern, traces of accelerant use, and the findings of what looks like glass and fabric, I'm saying this fire was deliberately set."

"This does not make me happy, bro."

The accompanying pout on his brother's face made Brody chuckle. "Can't say it's the highlight of my day, either. This is the fourth fire in the last few months. The first were small time stuff. But this? We're talking about somebody burning down an entire building. We're lucky there wasn't anybody inside."

Rafe pulled off his cowboy hat and ran his hand through his hair. "That thought has kept me awake. We need to figure this out, because I don't want a firebug running around in my county, putting people's lives at risk."

"I'm going to run these samples to Austin in the morning. I want to talk with somebody I know, get his advice. I haven't got a ton of arson expertise under my belt, since Shiloh Springs isn't exactly a hotbed of fire starters. I'll deliver the evidence to maintain the chain of evidence, but first, I have to call Ben Summers and tell him the bad news."

Rafe nodded. "Why don't you make the call from my office? Because knowing Ben, as soon as he hangs up from you, he's gonna be calling me, wanting to know what I'm doing to catch whoever burned down his barn. Might as well let him talk to both of us together."

"It's a dang shame, too. This is a great piece of land. Thankfully, the house is still standing, and didn't sustain any damage." Brody pointed with his thumb over his shoulder. "Do you remember—"

"When we snuck smokes up in the loft? How could I forget? I thought we were going to have to haul you to the hospital, you choked so hard. Your first and last cigarette, as I recall."

Brody laughed at the memory. "I remember Greg daring us. Said I was too chicken to smoke. Being chicken had nothing to do with it. I was too scared of what Ms. Patti would do if she caught me smoking. I think we sprayed half a can of air freshener on our clothes so she wouldn't know."

"Trust me, she knew."

Brody smiled at the memory. "I'm not surprised. She knew everything we ever did. Still does, though I try to pretend I have a few secrets she hasn't uncovered."

Rafe chuckled. "You keep thinking that, bro. Might help you sleep better at night."

Brody lifted the yellow caution tape and stepped underneath, walking past his brother toward his truck. He wasn't looking forward to the next couple of hours. Informing anybody when their property had been destroyed was never easy, especially when it was a friend. Gently placing the evidence bags on the seat, he turned toward Rafe.

"I'm gonna want to lock these in the safe at the sheriff's office until tomorrow. Need to keep the chain of custody intact and having them secured overnight at your office makes things a whole lot easier than taking 'em home with me."

"No problem, bro." Rafe studied him intently, and Brody started to feel like an insect with its wings pinned to a poster board in some kid's science presentation. Not a comfortable feeling.

"What?" *Well, shoot, that came out a lot louder than I intended.*

"I…never mind."

"Whatever it is, just ask already."

"Fine." Rafe blew out a long breath before he continued. "Is everything okay? You've been acting—I don't know— distant. Like you've got the weight of the world on your shoulders. Whatever it is, you know I'm here for you, right?"

Brody wasn't surprised by his brother's observation. Antonio had pretty much asked the same thing when he'd visited him in Austin, right before the whole thing with Serena. Which was probably a good thing too, because Antonio's sense of perceptiveness was on par with big brother Rafe when it came to family. As much as he wanted to talk to Rafe about his growing attraction for Beth, he wasn't ready.

"It's nothing, I swear. I've just had a lot on my plate lately, you know? Besides, you've got more than enough to take care of with your fiancée and your wedding plans. You don't need to worry about me."

Rafe didn't look convinced at his words. When he started to speak, Brody held up his hand. "I give you my word, if I need to talk, you'll be the first one I come to, okay?"

"You better," Rafe grumbled, before heading toward his

truck. "I'll meet you at the station."

Brody climbed behind the wheel of his own truck, started it, and followed his brother away from the blackened barn and toward town, wondering how long he could keep fooling himself about his feelings toward Beth. His feelings for his soon-to-be sister-in-law weren't going away; instead, every time he thought about her, he felt himself slipping further and further into a quagmire of unfamiliar emotions, with no way out.

Maybe his dad was right. It was time he did something about it.

Step number one, ask her out. Yep, sounded like a good start.

CHAPTER SIX

Beth walked out of the house onto the front porch, and sat on the front step, where she could keep an eye on Jamie while she took the call, her mind racing a thousand miles a minute. The last person in the world she'd expected to hear from was on the phone, currently holding while Beth geared up to talk to her former sister-in-law.

"Camilla, thanks for holding. We're right in the middle of moving into a new place, and I needed to check on Jamie."

She watched as Jamie spun around in circles on the small patch of front lawn, her arms spread wide as she twirled faster and faster, her infectious giggles making Beth smile. Jamie's happiness meant everything, and she'd do whatever it took to see her daughter never suffered from her father's misdeeds.

"How is Jamie? I miss her."

Beth heard the truth in Camilla's voice. It wasn't hard to believe Camilla missed her niece. She'd been the doting auntie, always willing to step in and babysit any chance she got. More often than not, whenever she visited, there was inevitably a new toy or trinket for Jamie. Camilla had been at the hospital when Jamie was born, had been there throughout the long, arduous hours of labor, and had been one of the first people in the room when she'd been allowed visitors.

A twinge of guilt hit. Was it right to paint her with the same brush as her brother? Logically, it wasn't fair, but didn't mean she automatically got a free pass. Truth be told, it was probably going to be a long time before Beth trusted anybody easily.

"Jamie's great. She's playing in the yard right now, and loving every minute."

"Good. Beth, I know I've said it before, but I honestly had no idea what Evan was doing. It's hard for me to wrap my head around the fact my brother tried to hurt Tessa. But I didn't know. I swear."

"I believe you, Camilla. You aren't your brother, and I'm trying really hard to get past what he did. That's why we're here in Texas. It's a brand-new start for me and Jamie. There are too many memories in North Carolina. Bad memories. Sad memories. We're happier here."

There was a catching sound on the other end, like Camilla had drawn in a ragged breath. "I understand. I guess I thought—assumed—you'd be coming back. I miss you and Jamie. I miss our friendship. When you married Evan, I felt as if I gained a sister, and I'd hate it if that was gone. Please, Beth, don't let what my brother did drive a wedge between us. The thought of never seeing you or Jamie again, it's tearing me apart inside."

"Camilla, I don't blame you because your brother is a rotten—" Beth broke off before calling Evan a host of really nasty names. No matter how much she now despised the loathsome toad, she couldn't take her ire out on Camilla. Evan was responsible for his actions, not his sister, and he'd get exactly what was coming to him. If she had her way, he'd spend the rest of his rotten life behind bars, with a very large roommate named Bubba.

"Don't think you have to censure yourself because he's my brother. You can't possibly call him anything worse than I've already called him. Which is part of the reason I'm calling. I'm going to be in Texas. I've got some papers Evan needs to sign. I was hoping, maybe, I could stop by and see you and Jamie?"

Beth sat in stunned silence for a few seconds. If she was honest, she'd admit she missed seeing Camilla. After she married Evan, they'd grown closer, hanging out with each other, and spending girls' days shopping, getting mani-pedis, and gossiping. They had grown close as friends, and Beth had looked at Camilla like a second sister. Even Tessa liked Camilla, often joining them on their girls' spa days.

"I'd like that, Camilla. I know Jamie misses you."

"Thank goodness! I was hoping you'd let me come and visit. I'm flying to Houston in two days, and renting a car. According to the internet, it's only a couple of hours' drive, barring bad traffic."

"Definitely count on traffic being horrible in Houston, especially downtown. The roads in the big cities always seem to be under construction in Texas. Otherwise, the trip's not too bad. Since you're driving, it'll take four, maybe four and a half hours, to get to Shiloh Springs. Want me to send you directions?"

"That's okay, I made sure the car I reserved has a GPS, so I shouldn't have any trouble finding you. I'll call and get more specifics once I'm actually in your little town, though."

"Sounds like a plan. You'll stay with us while you're here."

Camilla started to protest and Beth cut her off. "No sense staying in a hotel when I've got two bedrooms here. That's settled. Want to talk to Jamie before you go?"

"I'd love to."

Beth stood and started down the porch steps when she spotted Jamie edging closer to the street. Instead of panicking, which was her first instinct, she called out, "Jamie, come here. There's somebody who wants to talk to you."

Jamie raced across the grass, her small sneakers making barely a sound as she ran. With the vigor of youth, she bounced on her heels in front of Beth, a huge grin on her face. "Somebody wants to talk to me, Mommy?"

Beth smiled indulgently. "They sure do, sweetie." She handed her cell phone to her daughter.

"Hello?" She watched Jamie's smile widen, her blue eyes sparkling with delight. "Aunt Milla! We moved into a new house today! It's awesome. It used to belong to Aunt Tessa, but she's getting married, I mean married, and I get to be a flower girl. She says I'm big enough. I get a special new party dress, and I get to throw flowers, and all the people will be looking at me because I'm important."

Whatever Camilla said on the other end of the phone caused Jamie to squeal with laughter. Beth's heart melted, watching her daughter smiling and laughing and playing, as if she didn't have a care in the world, which was how it should be. It wasn't fair her life would be forever tainted by her father's actions, but for now she was sweet and innocent and naïve to the vagaries of the world, and Beth wanted to keep it that way for as long as she could.

"Mommy, Aunt Milla wants to say bye." Jamie held out the phone, her tiny hand barely able to wrap around the sides. "Here."

"Stay on the grass, Jamie." Beth brought the phone to her ear. "She's very excited about Tessa's upcoming wedding."

"I heard. Sounds like Tessa found the man of her dreams, and I couldn't be happier. She deserves somebody to love her for the wonderful woman she is. Honestly, I never liked Trevor, and couldn't understand why she dated him."

Beth almost rolled her eyes at Camilla's words. "Truthfully, neither can I. I never told her I didn't like him. There was something about him I didn't trust. Turns out I should have believed in my instincts. He's as bad as—"

Camilla sighed. "You can say it. He's as bad as Evan. Over the last few months, I've come to realize my brother isn't the man I believed him to be. I practically worshipped him when we were growing up. He was always so...perfect. Guess it's hard finding out your idol has feet of clay."

"I'm sorry. I never stopped to think how Evan's actions impacted you."

"It doesn't matter, as long as I know everything between us is still okay. Anyway, I'll see you in a couple of days, and we'll catch up on everything. Give Jamie a big hug for me. Love you guys!"

"Love you too. See you soon."

She disconnected the call and slid the phone in her pocket. It would be nice to see Camilla again, and while she was still furious with Evan, deep inside it didn't feel right to exclude the rest of his family from Jamie's life. Blaming them for her ex-husband's actions wasn't fair, but she also wasn't a fool. She'd watch out for her daughter. Jamie was the center of her world, and nothing and nobody was going to harm her. Not while Beth still had breath in her body.

"Come on, Jamie. We've got work to do if we want to have beds to sleep in tonight."

"Yay! I love it here, Mommy. Is Aunt Tessa coming to spend the night?"

Beth smiled, running her hand over the top of her daughter's head. "No, baby, Aunt Tessa is going to be sleeping at the Big House with Douglas and Ms. Patti until she gets married, remember? It's just you and me living here, kiddo. Now, come on, let's go make the beds."

Jamie bounded through the front door with all the enthusiasm of a four-year-old, and Beth envied her ability to adapt to new situations. Change wasn't easy, but sometimes taking the easy way out wasn't the answer. Walking the harder path meant forging a new life, one where she didn't risk her heart ever again. Especially when her heart kept telling her it wanted one tall, sexy Boudreau named Brody.

CHAPTER SEVEN

B rody pulled in front of the sheriff's station at the crack of dawn. Might as well get some work done, since he'd barely slept the night before. And the few precious hours he did sleep had been filled with dreams of Beth. Why couldn't he keep her out of his thoughts? Now she was haunting his dreams, leaving him irritable and unfulfilled.

He hadn't even stepped out of his truck before Rafe's pickup pulled up, parking behind his. Figured his brother would be in early, too. From the time he'd been elected county sheriff, Rafe took his job seriously, working extra-long hours, making sure the good citizens who'd elected him were never in doubt about his commitment to keeping them safe and secure in their homes.

"Morning, bro." Rafe held up two cups of coffee from the little place that had opened up across from Daisy's Diner a few months ago.

Brody grabbed one out of Rafe's hand and took a long drink. "You are a lifesaver."

"Figured you'd be in early to pick up the stuff from the Summers' place and drive it into Austin. A good dose of caffeine seemed in order."

Together they strode through the front door and headed toward Rafe's office. The evidence was locked up tight in the office safe, one less thing Brody had to worry about. He'd contacted the lab in Austin, notifying them he'd be bringing in multiple evidentiary items for processing from a suspected arson scene.

"Until I've got confirmation of arson at the Summers' place, can you have Dusty and a couple of the other deputies drive by and make sure nobody's out there messing with the barn? I doubt anybody will, but just in case."

"I've already talked with Dusty. He's on duty this afternoon. He'll make a sweep by there." Rafe shook his head. "I'm still trying to wrap my brain around somebody intentionally setting fire to that old barn. I mean, what's the point? Nobody's lived on the farm for years, and even before that, it wasn't more than an empty shell. Some nice wood, true, but other than that? Not a whole lot of value."

"I'm waiting to hear back from Ben or Greg Summers to see if there's insurance on the house, the barn, and the land. Routine in any fire. The owner's always suspect number one."

"I get it. I can't picture old Ben burning down his own property. Before his wife took ill, he put so much pride and hard work into his place. It's a real shame."

Brody perched on the corner of Rafe's desk, knee bent. "Greg never wanted the farm. He prefers living in the city.

Says he loves the excitement of the hustle and bustle of all the people, the energy. Personally, I don't see the appeal. Feel like I can't breathe when I'm away from Shiloh Springs for too long. I can handle a few days, maybe a bit longer, but then I start feeling claustrophobic. Give me a small town any day."

"Me, too."

"Anyway, thanks for the coffee. I need to hit the road. I told the laboratory I'd have the collected evidence to them first thing. Then I'm meeting Antonio for lunch. He's in Austin for the rest of the week. Apparently, Derrick Williamson's got another special case he wants Antonio's help with."

Rafe moved around Brody, kneeling down to open the safe situated in the corner of his office. There was a big evidence room at the very back of the sheriff's station, where most evidence collected from criminal investigations was held, but this larger safe was used for items which needed special handling. Chain of custody was crucial when prosecuting, especially in cases where special circumstances could be mucked up with contamination, and having a locked safe with no outside access kept things on the up-and-up.

"Everything's exactly as you left it last night. Seal's unbroken." Rafe lifted the large sealed cardboard container from the safe and set it on his desk.

The night before Brody had processed, labeled, documented, and logged every single item he'd picked up at the Summers' barn. Some of them were trickier than others and required specific packaging for transport. Documentation was key in any investigation in providing vital clues, which might be overlooked with sloppy paperwork and poor collection of evidence. This morning, he'd printed out all the photos he'd taken inside and out of the Summers' barn, and made a copy of the digital video of the scene. Now it was a matter of getting it all to Austin, where people with more specialized skill sets than his would either confirm or deny his suspicions.

"Great."

"Just sign here," Rafe passed across a receipt of evidence form, and Brody signed and initialed all the appropriate places and handed it back. "I think that takes care of everything. You need anything else?"

Brody shook his head and picked up the box. "Nope, I'm good. I'll give you a call later."

"Tell Antonio Momma's expecting him home this week-end. She's planning a big celebration."

Brody chuckled and walked toward the office's open doorway. "I'll tell him, although he mentioned he'd be back for the weekend. Don't think he can stand being away from Serena much longer. It's almost sickening watching those two lovebirds all cozied up. Almost as bad as watching you and Tessa."

He ducked the wadded-up paper Rafe tossed at him.

"You're jealous because you haven't got somebody special."

Brody froze at his words for the slightest second, because they scored a direct hit. As much as he wanted Beth, he didn't have her—and probably never would.

"Nope, I'm still footloose and free, while you're about to be leg-shackled for the rest of your life. You ready to take that big step, bro?"

"Honestly? I can't wait to make Tessa my wife. Never believed I could feel so much for one woman. I wouldn't change a thing, because she's everything. Everything."

"You know I'm kidding, right? Tessa is the best thing that's happened to you. I haven't seen you this happy ever. If I believed in soulmates, I'd say you've found yours. Nobody deserves happiness more than you, bro. Grab it with both hands and hold on tight."

Rafe strode forward and clasped Brody's shoulder, squeezing gently. "You'll find the same someday soon. The right woman's out there, and when you meet her, you'll know."

Brody's thoughts flew immediately to Beth. Then he remembered what his father had said to him in the barn. That he should take a chance with her, see where it might lead. Maybe now would be a good time to ask Rafe how he'd feel about him dating Beth.

Before he could say a word, Rafe's cell phone rang. Glancing at the number, Rafe grimaced. "Looks like kids have been out at Grady's place again. I'm going to have to call, get this sorted out."

"I've gotta hit the road anyway. Talk to you when I get back."

Without another word, Brody walked to the front of the sheriff's station and waved at Sally Anne on his way out. His father's words replayed in his head. He almost—almost—turned around and walked back inside to tell Rafe about his feelings for Beth, but duty called.

When he got back, though, he promised himself two things. Number one, he'd tell Rafe how he felt about Beth.

And number two, he'd ask Beth out on a date.

Beth rose early, and lay in bed, thinking about all the twists and turns her life had taken in the last couple of years. The death of her parents had hit her hard. Harder than she'd let on, because she'd needed to be strong for Tessa. Her sister had been devastated when their parents both succumbed to carbon monoxide poisoning in the home where they'd grown up. It was quick and sudden and unexpected. She'd done her best to be the pillar both Tessa and Jamie needed, never allowing herself to process her own grief until months later. And she'd never told anybody about her suspicions her ex-husband might have had something to do with her parents' deaths, not until Tessa told her Evan all but came out and said he'd done something, when he was terrorizing her sister.

All for money. It seemed like everything in her life centered around money. The Crowley County bond. Her parents' life insurance. Even earlier, Evan's insistence they couldn't start a family until they were more financially stable. And look where that got her, up to her neck in debt with no clear way out. Not unless the courts performed some kind of miracle, because Evan certainly wasn't going to be able to deal with the bills he'd accrued, falsifying her identity and racking up mountains of finance charges and second mortgage and credit cards she hadn't know about.

Now here she was in Texas. A new state and a new start. She might be dirt poor at the moment, but she felt happier and freer than she had in more years than she liked to remember. Through everything that happened, her one ray of sunshine lay sleeping in her brand-new bedroom down the hall. Without Jamie, Beth wasn't sure where she'd be now. Probably a total wreck, sobbing in the corner, pulling her hair out.

A slight noise of the door opening alerted her seconds before a giggling, tumbling mass of little girl flung herself onto the bed. Jamie's squirming body climbed up next to her, and wrapped her arms around Beth's neck. Beth squeezed her back tight before brushing a hand through her daughter's messy blonde hair.

"Good morning, sunshine."

Jamie giggled, that infectious sound brightening Beth's morning. "Morning, Mommy."

"Did you sleep okay in your new bed, sweetie?"

Jamie gave a vigorous nod, her blue eyes blinking rapidly. "I sleeped all night."

"That's good. You ready for some breakfast?"

Jamie sat straight up in the bed, turning to face her. "Faffles?"

Beth dropped her head forward and cupped it with her hands. "Seriously? You've had waffles every morning. I could make you some eggs. Maybe some toast with jelly?"

The mournful look on her daughter's face was priceless. Beth bit her lower lip to keep from laughing aloud. She'd probably never understand her daughter's fascination with frozen waffles, but at least she was eating, so she couldn't complain too much.

"Alright, waffles it is. Come on, let's go plug in the toaster."

"Yay!"

Jamie climbed out of the bed nearly as fast as she'd climbed in, but Beth followed at a more leisurely pace. She had a lot to get done today, including another call with her attorney, trying to straighten out the debacle of her finances with the courts. Next on her list was updating her almost non-existent resumé. Though she'd worked while attending college, mostly part-time jobs, she hadn't worked much after marrying Evan. She crossed her fingers, hoping lack of experience didn't come back to bite her in the butt.

She paused in the hall, glancing toward the living room

on her left. The warm colors, the soft leather, the darker wood pieces were all things she might have chosen herself, and she couldn't help the surge of warmth thinking about sharing similar taste with the man who seemed to occupy her thoughts more and more frequently.

"Mommy, are you coming?" Jamie's voice from the kitchen pulled her from her thoughts, and she turned right, heading through the opening. Boxes still lined the floor, pushed back against the walls so they wouldn't be tripped over. Another thing on her ever-growing list of things to do today. Finish unpacking.

"If you'll get the waffles out of the freezer, I'll get the plates and silverware, okay?"

"Yes, ma'am."

Within a few minutes, they had breakfast on the table, and Beth had a steaming cup of coffee in her hands. She pulled the belt of her robe tighter and leaned against the counter, adding a spoonful of sugar to her cup. Her brow creased at the trilling sound coming from her pocket, indicating a text. It was from Brody.

Hope you're settling in. I have to head to Austin this morning. You need anything, contact Rafe or Momma.

Well, that was unexpected. Warmth spread through her, and as much as she wanted to blame it on the coffee, she knew that would be a lie. Thinking about Brody almost made her feel like a schoolgirl again with her first crush. Which was ridiculous. She was a grown woman. A mother, not some adolescent teen, yearning for her first boyfriend.

Really, what's wrong with me thinking about another man? I'm not married. Not anymore. And things weren't all sunshine and roses when I was. Is it really so bad, thinking about wanting to be with Brody? I wonder if he's as curious as I am about this heat between us, or am I just imagining it? Or am I a fool for thinking there's something there and it's all in my head?

"Mommy, your faffles are getting all mushy from the syrup."

"Eww, yucky. I'm gonna eat them anyway." Beth smiled at her daughter, her empty plate in front of her. "Unless you want them." At Jamie's enthusiastic nod, she passed her plate across the table, then slid into the seat across from her and watched Jamie demolish the soggy mess, eating them so fast she wondered if her daughter had inhaled them without chewing.

"All done."

"I see. Go wash your face and brush your teeth. And wash your face good because you've got syrup all over your chin."

Her daughter raced from the room, and Beth realized she still held her cell phone in her hand. Touching the screen, Brody's text appeared, and she read it through again, not sure what she was looking for. Some secret subliminal message, or underlying declaration of desire. Ugh, she was being ridiculous, reading something into a kind gesture.

Except, maybe she wasn't. Maybe this was the universe

sending her a sign she needed to get off her keister and make the first move. Because frankly she was tired of being alone. She adored her baby girl, but sometimes she craved, she needed, somebody to hold her. To wrap their arms around her and let her simply lay her head on their shoulder and be.

Taking a deep breath, she punched in Brody's number, and hit call.

CHAPTER EIGHT

B rody arrived just outside the Austin city limits when his phone rang. Without bothering to check the caller ID, he hit the answer button. He'd connected the Bluetooth to his truck, so he'd have handsfree calls, one of the features he liked about his truck. A quick tap of a button on the steering wheel, and he could talk to anybody.

"Hello."

"Brody? Um, hi, it's Beth. I hope I'm not calling too early."

His gut tightened at the breathy quality in her voice. The sexy whispery rasp did something to his insides. An image of her, disheveled from sleep, eyes half-closed, and her hair tousled flashed through his mind, and he swallowed at the thought of her lying in bed talking to him.

"No, I've been up a couple of hours. Is anything wrong?"

"Everything's fine. Jamie and I have been up a while, too. She's already had her breakfast, and I'm on my second cup of coffee."

Brody smiled. "Lemme guess. Frozen waffles?"

"Not too much of a stretch there, Brody. Yes, she got

frozen waffles. Again."

"Nothing wrong with knowing what she likes and asking for it."

He heard Beth's sigh. "She definitely isn't shy about making her preferences known. I've promised her she can pick out the colors she wants for her new bedroom. I checked with Ms. Patti, and she said it would be okay to paint any of the rooms. Jamie and I are going to head to the paint store later this morning, so she can pick out exactly what she wants. I hope she doesn't pick some outlandish color. Heaven help me if she wants sparkles on her walls."

He could tell from her voice Beth was smiling, the happiness in her tone evident even over the miles separating them. "If you pick the color, I'd be happy to help you paint Jamie's room. Whenever you're ready, that is. Except today. I'm on my way to Austin."

There was a beat of silence and then another before she answered. "Brody, you've done so much for us already, I can't ask—"

"You didn't. I volunteered. I like helping out. I'm pretty good with a paintbrush and roller, had quite a bit of experience, so there's that."

"If you're sure it's not an imposition, I'd love the help."

Brody glided to a stop at an intersection, watching the traffic lights. Hearing Beth's voice made him wish he was back in Shiloh Springs, instead of an hour and a half away. He almost groaned when he noted the orange signs, indicating construction ahead on the road he needed to take to get to the Texas DPS Forensic Arson Laboratory, where he needed to drop of the evidence bags, and turn in the report of his findings.

"How about this weekend? I've got Saturday off. Bet we can get Jamie's room knocked out in no time."

"Actually, Saturday would probably be good. Today we're going to get Jamie registered for pre-kindergarten. I don't want her falling behind, especially with the move. I've been working with her, but it's not the same."

Brody chuckled, thinking about Beth and Jamie meeting with the kindergarten teacher. Mrs. Gleason had been teaching her little darlings, as she liked to call them, for longer than he'd been alive. She likened herself to being a second grandmother to all the kids. The children adored her, too, which made their parents very happy.

"Jamie will love Mrs. Gleason. I bet she'll have her wrapped around her little finger by the end of the first day."

"You know the kindergarten teacher? What am I saying, of course you do. You Boudreaus know everybody in Shiloh Springs, don't you?"

"I keep forgetting you're from the big city. I've lived most of my life here, so naturally I know most of the folks hereabouts. Mrs. Gleason has a way with the kids; you'd call it the magic touch. She's like the Pied Piper of the local munchkins. Jamie will be in good hands, I promise."

Brody heard a rustling sound, followed by Jamie's voice.

"Mommy, who you talking to?"

"I'm talking to Brody."

Her response was followed by a loud squeal. "Can I talk to Uncle Brody, Mommy?"

Seconds later, Jamie's voice asked, "Uncle Brody, you know what?"

"What, honey bear?"

"Mommy's taking me to school today. I went to school before, when we lived in the other place. Then I didn't go anymore. Now, I get a new teacher, and a new class. Do you think they have a lot of kids there? I really like having lots of kids to play with, and do art with, and write my numbers."

Brody felt his smile grow bigger. Jamie's enthusiasm for everything was infectious, and every time he saw her, she raised his spirits and lightened his heart. "I know your new teacher. Her name is Mrs. Gleason and she's really nice. And, yes, there will be lots of kids for you to play with. Your class is in a building with lots of big rocks on the outside, and a bright red roof made of metal."

"It has a roof of metal? I don't think I've ever seen one. I love red. It's pretty. Mommy, Uncle Brody says the place where school is has a metal roof and it's red. Can I paint my room red?"

"Red? Are you sure? Why don't we wait until we go to the paint store this afternoon and look at all the colors? You might see a different one you like better."

"Okay, Mommy. Uncle Brody, I gotta go finish getting

dressed. I love you."

The vice grip around his heart tightened at her casually stated words. He'd grow to adore the sweet little sprite over the past few months, with her golden curls and big blue eyes, and her caring and loving disposition. Jamie was one of those children who never met a stranger, and her larger-than-life personality encompassed everyone she touched.

"Love you, too, honey bear."

"Thanks, Brody. Seriously, a red metal roof? You might as well have waved a scarlet cape in from of her and said pick me, pick me." The amusement in Beth's voice played like music to his senses. He loved her sense of humor, which surfaced more and more lately, as she settled into her new life in Shiloh Springs.

"Not my fault if she wants a red room. Maybe you can talk her into a red blanket instead. Or one of those ruffled pillow things." He maneuvered his truck into the far-right lane, merging with the excruciatingly slow-moving traffic, which was down to one lane. At this rate, it'd be another hour before he hit the lab.

"Good luck with that," he heard Beth mutter.

"Beth, was there a reason you called? Not that I don't enjoy hearing your lovely voice first thing in the morning, but…"

"Oh, right. I just wondered if…maybe…that is," he could hear her take a deep breath, before she continued. "Would you like to go out with me sometime? For dinner?"

Wait, she was asking *him* out? He'd made up his mind to ask her out when he got home this evening, yet here she was, beating him to the punch.

"Yes."

"Okay. Good. Right." Now she sounded flustered. He didn't even attempt to fight his grin, smiling so big it almost hurt his cheeks. Had she expected him to turn her down? Like that was going to happen ever.

"When would you like to go out for this dinner?"

"Well, I'd thought about tonight, but since you're out of town—"

He cut her off before she could finish. "Tonight is good. I'll be heading back to Shiloh Springs after I drop off some stuff at the lab and turn in my reports on the Summers' fire. I should be home before six."

"Oh. That will work. How about we meet at Daisy's Diner at seven?"

"Beth, do you really want our first date to be in the middle of town, where everybody's going to be up in our business?" He'd grown up with the folks of Shiloh Springs, and while he loved them all, they did tend to get nosy. Not in a malicious way, it was simply because they cared. But for his first alone time with Beth, he wanted something a little more...intimate.

"I didn't think of that. Where would you suggest, Brody? You're more familiar with what's good around here. I'm still figuring out where stuff like the grocery store is." Her laughter was a beautiful thing, and he was so distracted he almost missed his turn. Waving a half-hearted apology to the driver he'd cut off, he drove another block before answering.

"If you don't mind a bit of a drive, I know a nice place. Quiet. Good food. Peaceful atmosphere. Sound good?"

"It sounds perfect."

"I'll pick you up at seven then." He pulled the car into the parking garage and quickly found an open spot. "No arguments, I'll drive."

"No argument. I'll see you tonight. Bye, Brody."

He hung up the phone and drew in a ragged breath. Images whirled around in his head with rapid-fire quickness. Beth laughing. Beth smiling. Beth standing in the moonlight, its subtle shadows highlighting her beauty. Tonight, he'd finally have her alone. Explore these feelings that kept him awake far too many nights, fantasizing about the intriguing, yet elusive woman.

He couldn't wait.

Evan hunkered down in the trunk, cursing when his cramped knees hit something sharp. It was black as pitch, and stifling hot. A trickle of sweat ran down his spine and he cursed again. Stuffed into the trunk of this tiny car almost made staying in his cell seem tolerable. Almost. Nothing on this earth equaled being caged like a beast, confined day in and day out with no way of doing anything about it.

Axel's plan had gone off without a hitch. If he didn't know better, Evan would think his cellmate had escaped from prison before, but he knew he hadn't, not with as much moaning and complaining the guy did on a daily basis. Axel talked about how he and his old lady plotted and planned for months how to get away if he was ever arrested again. When he'd ended up back behind bars, they'd started implementing their getaway. Evan was grateful the muscle-bound oaf had let him come along for the ride.

Axel and his woman were headed for the border. Lots of fun in the sun, that's all he'd talked about incessantly. Claimed he was going to live life free and easy on the Mexican Riviera. How he planned to do that Evan wasn't sure, since he knew Axel didn't have two nickels to rub together when he'd been tossed into the cell with him.

At least he's getting to ride inside the crappy car. It was little more than a rust bucket on wheels from its looks, but the engine purred like the proverbial kitten. Evan didn't care if it was a clown car from a three-ring circus. As long as it got him away from the prison and closer to getting his rightful payback, he'd stay inside this coffin on wheels.

It seemed like an eternity passed before Evan finally felt the car slow. The sound of gravel crunching was accompanied by the thump, thump, thump of the tires riding over something bumpy on the road. With a shudder and a lot of shimmying, the car finally eased to a stop. Then there was nothing but silence. Interminable silence which seemed to go on forever. He couldn't even hear a whisper from the passengers inside the vehicle, and his heartbeat sped up. Surely Axel wouldn't leave him locked inside the trunk and take off, would he? The acrid taste of bile rose in his throat at the thought, and he willed himself not to throw up. No, he wasn't going to die in the confines of a crappy compact foreign car.

Using what little room remained, he scooted and shifted around, contorting his body in ways he'd never imagined possible, until he got his feet braced against the car's back seat. Hauling his knees to his chest, he tucked them as tight as he could, and took a deep breath, ready to kick out toward the seat. Holding his breath, he unleashed his strength, his feet connecting with the heavy covering with a solid thunk. Nothing. It didn't budge, not even an inch.

Before he could pull his feet back for another kick, the trunk above his head flew open, and warm air and light filled the cramped space. Rolling over onto his back, he dragged in wonderful fresh air. Axel choked out a laugh, before reaching in and grabbing Evan's hand.

"Sorry, dude. Had to make sure nobody spotted us."

"Easy for you to say. You weren't the one stuck inside a cracker box without any air."

Axel rolled his eyes and slammed his hand against Evan's shoulder. "Wuss. I wasn't exactly riding in high style, you know. That hump in the middle of the floor in the back is a real pain in the—"

"Yeah, right. Where exactly are we?"

"Humble. About half hour, maybe forty-five minutes from Houston. Baby's gassing up the car. Should only take a second. Enough time for a bathroom break if you need it."

Evan straightened and rubbed his back, easing the soreness from being confined in such a tight space. Looked like it was time to say *adios* to Axel and head out on his own. Mexico didn't play into his plans, not yet. No, by the time he'd finished dealing with his traitorous witch of a wife, he'd head someplace where he could relax. Some place without extradition treaties, since he was now an escaped felon.

He wasn't going back behind bars ever again. The money he'd socked away for a rainy day was sitting in the bank, waiting for him. He'd been smart enough to put it under a different name, one nobody could even guess at. It wasn't nearly enough, not yet. But, before he was through, he'd have the funds to retire in style, and lounge on the beach and drink all the Mai Tais he wanted.

"Listen, Axel, I appreciate everything you've done, but I think splitting up's the best option here. The cops are going to be looking for two escaped prisoners, a black guy and a white guy. You'll have a better chance if it's you and your girl. With me being alone, well, they won't be expecting that." *I hope.*

"Wait…what? Dude, that's not the plan. All three of us are supposed to head south of the border. Mexico. Cops ain't looking for three people, either."

"I've been thinking about this a lot, and it's better this way, I swear. Besides, I've got some unfinished business I need to take care of before I can relax in the Mexican sunshine."

Axel simply shook his head. "It's your funeral, dude. You know where me and my lady will be hanging, if you change your mind."

"I'm gonna take you up on that. Just need to finish what I started first."

Axel yanked him in for a hug, and Evan cringed, even as he pounded the other's back. Yeah, he really needed to hit the road before things got any more awkward. He wasn't looking at being any part of Axel's extracurricular activities. Taking a step back, Evan finally noted what was in Axel's outstretched hand.

"Take these. They'll probably be too big, but they'll do until you can find something else. Can't have you running around in those," Axel gestured toward Evan's prison uniform. "You need cash? I ain't got much, but I can float ya a bit."

He didn't want to take Axel's money, but he'd be a fool to walk around strapped for cash, not even able to buy a meal. "That'd be awesome. I'll pay you back, I swear."

"Don't sweat it. Pay it forward when you can, help somebody else out. Anyway, my girl's headed this way, so we're outta here. Peace, my brother."

"Take care of yourself, Axel. Thanks for getting me out of that hellhole."

He stood, watching until the car drove out of sight, before heading toward the restroom with the clothes and cash. Making quick work of shedding the loathsome uniform, he wet and slicked back his hair, and scrubbed the grime of the trunk from his body as best he could do in the miniscule sink. Donning the T-shirt and jeans, he shoved the money in his pocket, and headed into the gas station's convenience store, and bought a map.

It took less than a minute to locate his destination.

Shiloh Springs, Texas.

CHAPTER NINE

Beth nibbled on her thumbnail and stared at the clothes laid out on her bed, a knot of dread in the pit of her stomach. What was she doing? She hadn't been on a date in…forever. Not since she'd married the ratfink ex. They'd never done date nights. Shoot, they'd barely spent quality time with each other once Jamie was born. Now, she'd jumped off the deep end and invited Brody on a date. A date! Maybe this was a dream, and she'd wake up and realize it was all in her imagination.

She reached for her forearm and pinched. Ouch! Nope, not a dream. Somehow, moving into Tessa's old cottage had jumpstarted her libido, and she'd given into temptation, and its name was Brody Boudreau.

"What ya doing, Mommy?"

Beth glanced toward her daughter, who stood in the bedroom's doorway, her head cocked to the side.

"I'm trying to decide what I'm going to wear."

"Why can't you wear what you got on?"

Beth wanted to laugh, because her daughter's question was said in such a serious tone. Jamie was too young to understand the ins and outs of fashion, especially dating attire. Not that she was any kind of expert. Jeans and a shirt had pretty much encompassed her entire wardrobe when she'd been dating her ex. She wanted to look nice tonight, but not like she was trying too hard.

"Aunt Tessa's here." Jamie made the announcement and proceeded to run down the hall, toward the front door. Ever since Beth had told her she'd be spending the night with her Aunt Tessa, Jamie had been a bundle of uncontained energy, over-the-moon excited to get to have a sleepover at the Big House. If she didn't know better, she'd swear those Boudreaus were spoiling her child. Oh, who was she kidding? They were totally treating Jamie like a pampered princess.

"Hey, Sis." Tessa sauntered through the bedroom door, her eyes instantly zeroing in on the stack of dresses, jeans, and tops. "What's going on?"

"I'm trying to figure out what I'm going to wear tonight."

Tessa's eyes narrowed, and she studied Beth intently. "You never mentioned when you called and asked me to watch Jamie what you were doing." Then her mouth dropped open for a second before she whispered, "Don't tell me. You've got a date? You've got a date!" Her voice got louder with each syllable, until she was nearly yelling by the end.

"It's nothing serious, Tessa. Just dinner between friends, that's all."

Tessa snorted. "You're not fooling me for a second. Spill. Who's the lucky guy? Give me all the deets."

Beth picked up a pale blue sheath and held it up to her chest. "There are no deets. Simply dinner as a thank you."

"Still not buying it. You haven't shown an interest in any guy since moving to Shiloh Springs. Unless...no, I don't believe it."

"What?"

Tessa's body practically quivered on the bed, and Beth rolled her eyes, before tossing the blue dress back on the bed, and picking up a soft peach-colored blouse with tiny buttons down the front and lace edging around the collar. From the corner of her eye, she watched Tessa, her expressions ranging from astonished to amused.

"Please, oh, please...tell me you're finally going to put Brody out of his misery and go out with him."

The blouse she held slipped from her fingers and she stared at her sister. "What are you talking about?"

"Sis, are you blind? Or just out of practice? Brody is definitely interested in getting to know you." She waggled her brows in an exaggerated fashion. "The guy is totally besotted."

Images of Brody raced through her head, playing like a slideshow. His cheeky grin. His crooked half-smile when he watched Jamie. Could she have missed all the signs? Granted, she'd been careful not to give out any mixed signals, but Brody hadn't given any indication he was interested in more than being her friend, had he?

"I think you're seeing things that aren't there. Brody and I are simply friends."

"Yeah, right. I might buy that if I wasn't sitting in the middle of your entire wardrobe, with you trying to find the perfect outfit to wear *on your date*." Tessa lightly fingered the edge of a knit top, the vibrant red color striking against the majority of pastels that made up the mainstay of Beth's wardrobe. Never one to stand out, she tended to wear the more subtle, subdued palate. Along with a couple pair of black pants and a black skirt, that comprised the extent of her wardrobe. That brilliant red top had been her one splurge, but she'd never had the nerve to wear it.

"I'm right, though. You're going out with Brody?"

Beth drew in a deep breath before answering. "Yes. I called him this morning."

Tessa bounced on the mattress. "You actually called him? That's kinda awesome, Sis. It's about time you put that jackass Evan behind you and got on with your life. You deserve the best, and Brody is definitely one of the good guys."

"Look, Sis, don't make more of this than what it is, dinner between two friends. I don't know if I'm ready for anything more than that. It's too soon. Think about it, the ink is barely dry on the divorce papers—"

"Don't hand me that bull hockey. We both know Evan is a ratfink, no good louse, and you shouldn't waste another minute thinking otherwise. Notice I'm using my polite words here, instead of cursing him, which truth be told, I've done many, many times. He's the one who cheated, practically the whole time you were married. Then he planned to kill you. Shoot, tried to kill me and Rafe." Tessa rose from the bed and wrapped her arms around Beth. "Please, Beth, don't let him steal your happiness. You and Jamie have started over. It's a brand-new life. A new beginning. Be open to new experiences. Be brave. Be the sister I remember, the one who looked life in the eye and smiled. I want to see your smile again."

She sniffled, fighting back the tears that threatened. Tessa had been there for her through the horrendous aftermath of Evan's betrayal. There were times, she was convinced, she'd never have made it through without her. Plus, she was right, she couldn't allow Evan to steal one more moment of her joy. Jamie deserved better. She deserved better, too. Evan made his choices, and now he could deal with the consequences, but that didn't mean she had to bury herself in regret or shame. What happened rested squarely on his shoulders.

Realizing she'd been carrying around a gigantic burden from Evan's perfidious behavior, it felt like an epiphany, the shedding of the weight of guilt and remorse for not realizing sooner what he'd been doing to her and her family. No more. Today, she started living again.

"I promise things will be different. I'm done hiding. Done paying for something I didn't do and had no control over. How about you help me choose an outfit for tonight?"

Tessa smiled and cupped her sister's cheek. "There she is, the sister I remember. The fighter." She turned to the bed. "Where are you going tonight?"

Beth shrugged. "I have no idea. I suggested Daisy's, but Brody wanted someplace else. He's going to pick me up at seven."

Tessa tapped a finger against her lips. "Hmm, since we don't know formal or casual, wear the red top and the black pencil skirt. It's classy, but not too fussy. Perfect for dressing up or down."

"The red one? Are you sure it's not too…I don't know…flashy?"

"Nonsense. You'll look gorgeous in it, and knock Brody on his keister. Here," she picked up the skirt and the top and shoved them into Beth's hands. "Pair this with your black boots, and you'll look amazeballs, Sis. Go get changed, and I'll help you with your makeup. I'll check on Jamie while you dress."

Beth hugged Tessa tight. "You are the best sister in the world."

Tessa chuckled. "I know. Get dressed." She left the bedroom, and Beth smiled at her bellowed call for Jamie. Turning, she headed for the bathroom to change, anticipation swirling inside along with excitement, feelings she hadn't experienced in a long time. Too long. She couldn't wait to see Brody.

Brody cursed for what had to be the dozenth time since he'd left Austin. Everything that could possibly go wrong did, until he'd been ready to shoot the next person who complained, questioned, or delayed his leaving town. All through the morning, he'd replayed his conversation with Beth in his head. Finally—finally—his patience was about to pay off, because they had a *date*. He'd handled her with kid gloves, because he knew after the traumatic turn her life took, she wasn't ready to deal with anybody coming on too strong. Instead, he'd taken things slow and easy, had become her friend. Now, he was hoping she might be ready for more.

A loud pop sounded, and his truck yanked hard to the side. Tightening his hands on the steering wheel, he maneuvered to the shoulder of the road and climbed out. Cursed when he saw the shredded left front tire, the rim resting on the gravely dirt beside the two-lane road.

"Perfect. Just freaking perfect."

Reaching behind the driver's seat, he felt around for the spare tire kit, his fingers fumbling around, and finding nothing. Tilting the seat forward, he banged his fist on the seat, because it was easy to see the kit and jack were missing. *I'm going to kill Ridge.* When he'd been home, Ridge had a flat, and asked to borrow his jack, and promised to put it back when he finished. Apparently the jackass hadn't, and now Brody was stuck thirty minutes from home.

Whipping out his cell phone, he punched in Ridge's number. *He'd better answer his phone, or I'm gonna tear him a new one when I catch up to him.* The call went straight to voice mail after one ring, and Brody huffed out a long breath. Why? Why did this have to happen on one of the most important days in a long time?

A red Ford pickup eased to a stop directly behind him, and Brody glanced at the driver before a huge grin spread across his face. Somebody upstairs was looking out for him, because Liam sat behind the wheel. Walking back to his brother's pickup, he leaned on the open door.

"Bro, am I happy to see you. Got a flat, and Ridge apparently didn't return my jack after he borrowed it."

"No problem, I've got mine. Want a hand?" Liam's words were accompanied by a smile. "Good thing I headed home early today, or you'd be stuck waiting for Frank to come fix it."

"Appreciate the help. I need to get home and grab a shower. I've got plans tonight and really don't want to cancel."

Liam slid from the truck and reached behind the driver's seat, pulling out everything to fix Brody's flat. Between the two of them, they should be able to make quick work of changing it, and Brody would get back on the road before too much more time passed.

"Hot date, huh?"

Brody grunted as he looked under the back of his truck for the spare, then straightened, holding his hand out for the tools. "Yeah. I'm going out with Beth Stewart."

Liam whistled and bumped his shoulder against Brody's. "Whoa, seriously? You finally got off your butt and asked her out?"

"Nope. She asked me." Brody tried to hid his smirk, but wasn't sure how successful he was. "Called me this morning, out of the blue, and asked me to dinner."

"That's awesome. Maybe now you can both stop making goo-goo eyes at each other when you think nobody's watching."

Brody straightened to his full height and spun to face his brother. "What are you talking about?"

"Dude, are you oblivious or simply blind? You look at her like she is a roast beef dinner and you haven't eaten in days. She looks at you like you hung the moon and the stars. Frankly, it's getting kinda old."

"I thought I hid my feelings pretty well."

Liam slapped him on the back. "Don't forget, I've known you most of our lives. I've seen how you look at women, and I've seen how you look at Beth. There's no comparison. She does something to you none of the others did. It's about time you figure out if she's the one."

Brody knelt and began removing the lug nuts off the flat. "What if she is? The one, I mean? Won't it be weird, seeing as how her sister is marrying our brother?"

Liam shrugged and folded his arms across his chest. "Naw, I'm fine with it. Not saying some folks won't gossip. That's human nature, a little scandalous, a bit salacious.

Fodder for the rumor mill, especially in a small town like Shiloh Springs. Nobody in the family's gonna object, if that's what you're wondering. Anybody else says anything, they'll answer to us. And I doubt anybody wants to cross Momma."

Brody gave an expert flip of his wrist and pulled off the last lug nut. Pulling the flat off, he laid it on the ground and lifted the spare, shifting and turning it to fit into place, all the while considering Liam's words.

"She's been through a lot. It's a good thing her ex is behind bars, or I'd be tempted to hunt him down and teach him a lesson."

"Trust me, you're not the only one. I think Dad would be first in line behind you."

Their father had made his feelings clear on more than one occasion exactly what he thought of Evan Stewart and his actions toward Beth and Jamie. Though never when Tessa or Beth were within earshot. None of the men in the Boudreau clan disagreed with their father's assessment and his multitude of suggestions of what Stewart deserved. Personally, Brody wished he could get five minutes alone in a room with the other man.

Finished tightening the lug nuts, Brody released the jack and lowered the truck. Liam grabbed the flat and tossed it into the truck bed, and Brody gathered the tools and handed them back to his brother.

"Thanks. You're a lifesaver." He plucked at his sweat-soaked shirt. "I definitely need a shower now. I should have just enough time to get home and changed before picking up Beth."

"Where are you taking her?"

"Claudette's."

"Nice. I figured first date you should go someplace special, where you might get a bit of privacy," Liam chuckled. "Not something you're likely to get if you went anywhere in Shiloh Springs. The gossip mills would be running overtime before you even sat down."

"Which is why I vetoed Beth's suggestion of going to Daisy's. I want to spend a little private time with her. Just the two of us, you know?" Brody brushed his dirty hands on his jean-clad thighs. "Tessa's gonna watch Jamie for the night."

Liam quirked a brow and gave him a knowing grin. After giving Brody a slap on the back, he headed for his truck. "Have a good time, bro. You deserve it."

"Thanks. And thanks for the rescue."

"No problem. Call me tomorrow and let me know how it goes."

Brody waved as Liam pulled back onto the road, before climbing behind the wheel and starting his truck. A quick glance for oncoming traffic, and he was headed back toward Shiloh Springs and his date with Beth.

Nothing better ruin his plans for the perfect evening. Nothing.

CHAPTER TEN

It felt like a million butterflies had taken flight in her stomach as Beth watched through the front window as Brody's pickup truck pulled into her drive. Her hands clenched into fists, and she nervously opened and closed them several times, her breath caught in her throat. She'd been on pins and needles for the past half hour, fussing over and over with her hair, wondering if she had on too much makeup or not enough.

Tessa and Jamie left for their sleepover at the Big House right after Tessa had finished helping her get ready. Thinking about Jamie made her heart feel light. She'd adjusted beautifully since they'd come to Shiloh Springs, better than Beth could have hoped. Ah, the joys of youth. Nothing seemed to phase her daughter except, heaven forbid, they run out of frozen waffles. That catastrophe might be the end of the civilized world.

The knock on the door brought her thoughts flying back to Brody. *He's here. Standing on my front porch. Not with the rest of the Boudreaus hanging around. Not with a house full of people, chattering and futzing around. Alone. He's here to see me. Not me and Jamie. Me.*

Her stomach quivered, nerves fluttering deep inside, and she felt almost lightheaded. Which was ridiculous, she reminded herself. They were simply two friends going out to dinner. People did it all the time.

Except most people weren't Brody Boudreau.

Pulling open the front door, Brody stood on the other side, dressed in dark jeans and a white shirt open at the throat, hints of sun-bronzed skin peeking out. The dark cowboy hat he favored, the one he wore when he wasn't working at the fire station, covered his sandy-brown hair. A smile lit his face, reflected in his cognac-colored eyes, ones she could stare into for hours.

"Hi." Her voice crackled on the single word, and she swallowed.

"Evening, Beth." His slow perusal slid along her skin like a silken caress, and from his heated stare, she knew he liked what he saw. Boy, oh boy, was she glad she'd listened to Tessa's advice and worn the red top. His gaze paused for a long moment, studying her, and she couldn't miss the way his eyes seem to eat her alive, before slowly meeting hers.

"Would you like to come in?" There, that was better. At least the words didn't stick in her throat this time. She needed to pull herself together. Stop acting like she'd never talked to a man before. She could do this. Taking a step forward, she pushed open the screen door, and Brody stepped through. The creak from the hinges broke through the awkward silence.

"Remind me to fix that," Brody murmured, as he took off his hat, holding it casually at his side.

"Would you like something to drink before we leave?" She smoothed her sweaty palms against her skirt, wishing she could be suave and sophisticated, instead of a heaving bundle of nerves. Just her luck, getting ready to go out with the man of her dreams, and she was acting like the nerdy girl from high school, the one who never got asked out.

"Is everything okay? Did I do something wrong?"

Beth gave a nervous laugh. "Nothing's wrong. It's me. I…it's been so long since I went out on an actual date, it's like I can't remember how I'm supposed to act. It's stupid, I know."

"It's not stupid. It's simply different. Have you changed your mind—about wanting to go out? I'll understand if you want to call it off."

Beth's brain seemed to freeze at his words, before a thousand things sped through it, each one faster than the last. Had he changed *his* mind? Maybe he didn't want to go out with her, or worse, he looked at this as a pity date.

"Stop it."

"What?"

"No, this is not a pity date. Nothing could be farther from the truth. And I haven't changed my mind. I've wanted to take you out for ages."

Heat flooded Beth's cheeks when she realized she'd spoken her thoughts out loud. At least Brody wasn't fleeing out the door, even though she'd given him every excuse under the sun to run as far and as fast as his feet would carry him.

"I'm sorry," she whispered. "Things are such a jumble in my head right now. I'm the one who called you and asked you out. Then I had second thoughts. Heck, third and fourth thoughts. I really don't want to screw up our friendship."

Brody cupped her cheeks between his hands, his touch soft and gentle. "I've been looking forward to our dinner together ever since you called. I couldn't get out of Austin fast enough, wanting—no—needing, to get home because all I could think about was going out with you. Yes, Beth, we are friends. But who says being friends can't lead to something more if we want it to?"

Beth stared into his golden-brown eyes, wanting to lose herself in his gaze, because she knew he meant every word. Maybe she wasn't the only one drowning in desire. A heady mixture of desperation and excitement sizzled through her, and she barely bit back a moan. Her lips parted as Brody leaned in, holding her breath because she wanted this kiss. The warmth of his exhaled sigh against her skin had her eyelids closing in anticipation. This moment? This instant out of time? She'd dreamed of it for so long—their first kiss.

The loud trill of her cell phone broke the spell which mere seconds before held her frozen in place. Her eyelids flew open, and she automatically took a step back, the magic lost at the incessant ringing of her phone. Brody ran a hand through his hair, a guarded look on his face.

"You probably should get that."

"Um, yeah, I guess so." Her finger slid across the face of the phone. She didn't bother looking at the caller ID, because it didn't matter. Their special moment had disappeared like a puff of smoke on the breeze, and deep inside she couldn't help wondering if there'd ever be another.

"Hello?"

"Good evening, ma'am. Is this Beth Stewart?"

Still only half paying attention, she responded, "Yes, it is."

"Ms. Stewart, this is Deputy Warden Jackson over at Huntsville. We're sure there's no cause for alarm, ma'am, but I'm calling to inform you Mr. Evan Stewart escaped earlier today..."

The phone slipped from Beth's numb fingers, crashing to the floor. She heard Brody's voice calling her name, but the words were distant, muffled beneath the ringing in her ears. The words she'd heard reverberated in her head, repeating over and over. Evan escaped. Evan escaped. Evan escaped.

Jamie!

She had to get to her daughter. Protect her. Make sure she was safe. Every instinct screamed at her to run, run as far and as fast as her legs would carry her. Race away from Shiloh Springs, because Evan knew they lived there now. Find some place where Evan could never find them. The careful life she'd created for her daughter crumbled into a thousand brittle shards, charred and ruined, and she wasn't sure she could put them back together again.

Brody's arm snaked around her waist, which was good because her knees felt like limp noodles, ready to collapse beneath her. Her gaze centered on his face, reading the barely restrained anger as he spoke to the official from Huntsville. How could this happen? The illusion of safety she'd cloaked herself in lay in tattered ruins. Would she ever feel safe again?

With his arm tight around her, Brody led her to the sofa and eased her onto it, the whole time talking with the warden. His arm loosened from around her, and immediately she felt its loss. Without his touch, she felt encased in ice, cold and numb to everything around her. Staring down at her hands, she bunched her fingers into fists, marveling she could move them at all, because she felt frozen. Numb. Trapped in a cocoon of icy despair, because her illusion of happily ever after fragmented with one phone call. She'd deluded herself into thinking she had a shot, a chance at making a new life, finding a new love with Brody.

Her gaze lifted to Brody's as he knelt beside her, his strong hand wrapped around the cell phone. Now he'd realize it wasn't good to be around her. Nobody needed to be stuck with her. Her life was jinxed, it had been from the day she'd met Evan Stewart, and fallen for his lies and deceit.

"Sweetheart, they've got everybody looking for Evan.

They'll catch him. I promise, he's not getting anywhere near you or Jamie, okay? Let me call Rafe, find out what he knows."

"I need to see Jamie." She hated how her voice quivered, nearly cracking toward the end. She tried to sit a little straighter. This had to stop. She wasn't some crybaby, some weak, lily-livered wimp. When Evan had tried to manipulate her after he'd been arrested, she'd grown a backbone and stood up to him. Divorced him and moved on, making a new life for her and her daughter. She wasn't about to let him break her now. "She's going to be scared when she hears about her father."

"As soon as I talk to Rafe, we'll head to the ranch. Couple of minutes, tops."

She rubbed her upper arms, trying to feel warm again. Without a doubt, Brody was right. They needed to find out what Rafe knew, and take the appropriate steps to protect not only Jamie, but Tessa, too. Evan wasn't above going after her sister, since she'd been a huge part of him being behind bars.

"Do it. Because I want him as far away from my daughter as humanly possible. If we're lucky, maybe he grew a brain while he was incarcerated, and is across the border in Mexico."

Brody's crooked grin at her words made the invisible layer of ice surrounding her heart start thawing. Evan better watch his back, because if he was stupid enough to show up in Shiloh Springs, she'd be ready.

Hanging up after talking to the deputy warden, Brody's thoughts were spinning a mile a minute. He still didn't understand how Evan Stewart managed to slip through the cracks at Huntsville, but he was on the loose, with a full manhunt in progress. They'd been searching for several hours, the warden said, but he and his cellmate were in the wind. Apparently, they'd had outside help, and the police were looking for Evan's cellmate's girlfriend, but hadn't had any luck thus far.

Biting back a curse, he laid Beth's phone on the coffee table in front of her. He'd managed to get her seated while he'd finished the call, but knew she'd retreated into her thoughts. Didn't take a genius to figure out exactly what she'd do. The minute she got herself together, she'd head to the Big House, grab Jamie, and hightail it out of Shiloh Springs as fast as she could load herself and her daughter in their car. No, he wasn't about to let that happen, not if he could stop it.

He yanked his cell phone out of his pocket and hit speed dial for Rafe's number. He paced across the living room floor, agitated his brother didn't answer on the first ring.

"Hey, Brody, what's up?"

"Why didn't you call me the second you heard about

Stewart?" Brody's tone sounded overly harsh, but he was pissed, and didn't really care who knew it. He kept his voice low, because Beth didn't need to hear this conversation. She'd been blindsided by the news about her ex. Somebody better have some answers for him, ones that made more sense than the little he'd been able to pry outta the deputy warden. Otherwise, he might not be responsible for his actions.

"Stewart? Are you talking about Evan Stewart?"

"Why didn't you tell me he escaped? How come you don't have somebody watching Beth's house?"

"Whoa, hold on. What are you talking about?"

Brody took a deep breath, trying to quash down the rage coursing through him, which wasn't easy. Every second Evan was free meant Beth and Jamie were in danger. He might not be a cop, but he'd protect them both with his life.

He took another steadying breath, focusing on the facts. Rafe was a good sheriff; he wouldn't let anything happen to Beth or Jamie. His gut tightened at the thought of Beth's ex getting his hands on her, and literally saw red. "Beth got a call a few minutes ago from Huntsville. Apparently, Evan and another prisoner escaped this afternoon. Are you telling me you didn't know?"

"Son of a—no, I didn't know. Let me make some calls and get back to you." Rafe hung up before Brody could say anything else. He glared at his phone, fighting the compulsion to throw it against the wall. He couldn't; he needed to keep it handy in case Beth's ex showed up. If Stewart was smart, he'd be halfway to Mexico now, instead of heading toward Shiloh Springs. Stewart had to be certifiable if he thought he'd get anywhere close to Beth or Jamie.

"What did Rafe say?" Beth's words were spoken quietly, as if she felt the rage boiling beneath the surface, the seething anger needing an outlet. The thought of her in danger, he refused to give it any credence, because he'd lose his mind. She had enough to deal with without him loosing what little control he clung to. Reining his emotions back, cooling down the spike of adrenaline coursing through his veins, he moved over to sit beside her, and pulled her hands between his. They were icy to his touch.

Calm. You've gotta stay calm. Beth needs you in control.

"He didn't know anything about Evan. Nobody from the prison called him. He's trying to find out more information. Come here." Reaching for her, he pulled her against his side, and tucked her head against his shoulder. Felt her body trembling against his. Reaching along the back of the sofa, he lifted the crocheted afghan with one hand and wrapped it around her. "He'll call back as soon as he knows something. If Evan's smart, he'll head anywhere but Shiloh Springs. It's the first place anybody's gonna look for him."

"I know that in here," she pointed to her head. "But I can't trust him around Jamie. He won't hesitate to use her as a bargaining chip to get me to do anything he wants."

"He won't get the chance. Let me call the Big House, and put them on alert, just in case. The Boudreaus can circle the wagons and keep Jamie safe."

At her nod, he pressed the speed dial for home. His dad answered on the first ring. "Hey, Brody. I thought you were on a date with Beth."

"Change of plans. Beth got a call from Huntsville."

"What happened?" His father's tone went instantly alert, concern lacing his father's words. Douglas had dealt with more than his fair share of crises through the years, and Brody knew he'd protect Jamie with his life. There wasn't a doubt in his mind as soon as his father knew the situation, he'd round up the rest of Brody's brothers, and they'd do whatever it took to keep her protected.

"Evan Stewart escaped this afternoon." Brody let the stark words convey everything he felt, knowing his father would immediately grasp the gravity of the situation. As much as he wanted to rail at the unfairness, he couldn't, not with Beth sitting beside him, her nerves already frazzled and on edge.

"How'd he manage that?"

"I don't know, nobody's been exactly clear on the details. He apparently escaped with his cellmate a few hours ago."

"And they're just now letting us know? What'd Rafe say, because I know you talked to him before you called me."

"Nobody bothered to notify him either. First he heard of it was a couple minutes ago when I called him.

"How's Beth holding up?" Brody heard his mother's voice in his ear, and knew she'd snatched the phone away from his dad. "You bring her here right now, you hear me? If her ex shows up, we'll handle it." And there was the backbone of steel his mother possessed. Almost everybody underestimated her when they first met her. Barely over five feet, she looked like a breeze could blow her down. He and his family knew better. The woman was a dynamo wrapped in a delicate package. Nobody got the best of Patricia Boudreau. She'd raised more troubled, rebellious boys than most people dealt with in a lifetime, and she wrangled 'em into shape with one hand tied behind her back. Everyone in Shiloh Springs knew better than to cross Ms. Patti, as all the locals called her. Now that Tessa was marrying Rafe, she was family, and Beth and Jamie became honorary Boudreaus by default.

"That's my plan, Momma. Keep an eye on Jamie."

"She's in the kitchen with Dane and Nica."

"Nica's there?"

"Showed up this afternoon. Said she was taking a long weekend from classes. Now I'm glad she did, she can help keep Jamie occupied while we deal with this little problem."

Brody bit back a grin. His momma calling Evan Stewart a little problem—he'd bet good money on the outcome of seeing Evan go up against Patti Boudreau. Evan would be slinking back to Huntsville, begging them to let him back inside by the time she was finished with him.

"Brody?" Beth moved quietly to his side, her tiny hand resting on his arm, a question in her voice.

"It's okay, sweetheart. Dad and Momma are watching Jamie. Dane and Nica are keeping her occupied. Everything's going to be fine."

"I'll expect to see you here ASAP, son." Apparently his momma gave the phone back to his dad, because his voice was the next one he heard. "Antonio's supposed to be showing up in about an hour too. Maybe he can make some calls to his FBI contacts, find out anything the locals aren't telling us. I'll call him, tell him to bring Serena with him. Another female around to help Beth won't be a bad thing."

"Thanks, Dad. We're on our way."

He slid his cell phone into his pocket, and pulled Beth around to face him. Giving her a once over, she looked calmer, not as shaky as she'd been a few minutes ago.

"Jamie's safe?"

"She's surrounded by a house full of family, she's fine. Grab your stuff, we're heading there too. I'm texting Rafe, so he'll know where we are."

She grabbed her purse and walked to the door. "Let's go."

Brody walked her onto the porch, making sure the front door was securely locked behind him. A quick scan of the yard and street in front of the cottage didn't reveal anything suspicious, and he quickly helped Beth into the truck, before climbing behind the wheel.

Evan Stewart better hope the cops catch up to him before I do.

CHAPTER ELEVEN

Beth curled up in the overstuffed chair in the living room of the Big House, a crocheted throw wrapped around her shoulders. A hot cup of tea, clasped between both hands, remained untouched. Closing her eyes, she took a deep breath, trying to release some of the tension and anxiety knotted deep in her belly.

Brody drove them straight to his family's home. Rafe still hadn't called, so there hadn't been any more news about Evan or where he might be. She prayed he kept running in any direction, as long as it wasn't Shiloh Springs.

Jamie was tucked into bed, with Nica to keep her company. Nica volunteered to keep an eye on her, going as far as to suggest sharing her bedroom with her. Beth knew the Boudreaus would be supportive in a crisis, but she'd never imagined how much she depended on them. Ms. Patti had put out a call and rallied the troops, and now the house teemed with people. Antonio and Serena showed up mere minutes after she and Brody. Antonio had been on the phone since they'd arrived, contacting his FBI sources, and going through the legitimate channels to generate any information on her ex.

"Rafe's on his way." Ms. Patti eased onto the ottoman in front of Beth's chair. She reached forward and laid her hand on Beth's knee. "Can I get you anything, hon?"

Beth shook her head, and took of sip of the tea. Chamomile, hot and sweet, the way she liked it. Warmth spread through her, and she sipped again.

"Everything's going to be okay. They'll catch Evan and he'll be back in Huntsville before you know it. Plus, you've got a houseful of folks who'll keep you and Jamie safe." Ms. Patti leaned forward and whispered, "I hope they catch him before Brody gets his hands on him. Probably won't be enough left to lock in a cell if Brody or Rafe find him first. They've got a personal stake in making sure Evan gets exactly what he deserves."

Beth raised her head and stared at Ms. Patti, who simply shrugged, a conspiratorial smile on her lips. "What, I'm just saying what everybody else is thinking."

"I thought this nightmare was over when Evan went to prison. That I was finally free from the devastation he'd made of my life. Of Jamie's life. Now, I know it's never going to end. He's like the boogie man; he'll never really be gone. We're never going to be free of him."

"Hush. I don't want to hear you talk like that. Evan Stewart is simply a man. He's not a bigger-than-life ghoul, he's just a human-style monster. And if you've read any fairy tales, which I know you have because of Jamie, you know the monster can be slayed. Lucky for you, I happen to have a house full of monster slayers."

The corners of Beth's lips tugged in an involuntary smile, picturing Brody in a suit of shining armor, sword in hand, standing over a sobbing, cowardly Evan. "Thanks, Ms. Patti. I needed to hear that."

The front door swung open hard enough to slam against the wall, and Tessa swept through like a whirlwind, eyes frantic until they landed on Beth. Eyes filled with tears, she rushed across the living room and threw herself against Beth, hugging her so tight, Beth squeaked.

"Can't breathe."

Tessa's grip loosened a tiny bit, and she gave a watery laugh. "Sorry. Are you okay?"

Beth nodded and set down her empty teacup, glad she finished it before being hit by Tornado Tessa, or she'd have been wearing it.

"I'm fine. Jamie's asleep. Nica's keeping an eye on her."

"Good. How could this happen? I mean, I know people sometimes escape from prison in the movies, but real life? It's not right."

"I...we don't have any details yet. All I've heard is what Brody got from the deputy warden at the prison. Evan and his cellmate escaped, so they must have been planning it. They are pretty sure they got help from the cellmate's girlfriend."

Ms. Patti silently stood and motioned for Tessa to take

her place on the ottoman and headed for the kitchen. Beth glanced toward the opening between the kitchen and the living room, and saw Rafe standing there, his gaze intent on Tessa. Beth felt a bit envious at the look of love on his face. Not that she begrudged her sister having found the man of her dreams. It almost made her believe in happily ever after again. At least for everybody else.

"Any news yet?" She directed her question to Rafe.

He walked across the room and placed his hand on his fiancée's shoulder, giving it a gentle squeeze. "Not much. A state trooper talked to a gas station attendant, who thinks he spotted a couple of men and a woman who stopped for gas. One of them was dressed in prison garb—he thinks. One man and the woman drove off, leaving the third person behind. Unfortunately, he was unable to identify anybody from the photo lineup, so it's all guessing at this point, but they might have split up."

"Which means Evan's traveling alone?"

"It's only speculation at this point, Beth."

She wrapped the throw tighter around her, feeling the invisible chill teasing along her skin. Bile rose in the back of her throat, a feeling of lightheadedness sweeping over her. "He's coming here—to Shiloh Springs."

"There's no proof of that, but, yeah, I think you're right." He knelt beside her chair, his intent gaze locked with hers. "He's not getting anywhere near you or Jamie. We're all here. I've got deputies working around-the-clock watching the main roads into town. Antonio's got the FBI searching. Evan's not stupid. He has to know you're protected."

"He's not stupid, but he is vain. He'll take it as a challenge to get the best of you, because you beat him before. I hurt his pride when I divorced him and took his daughter away. To his thinking, what does he have to lose by coming after me...us?"

"Stop it." She hadn't heard Brody come into the room, but the vehemence behind his comment had her straightening in the chair. "Your ex isn't getting near you or Jamie. Not now, not ever."

There was a finality in his words, a conviction which made her feel safe. For the first time since she'd gotten the call from the prison, Beth felt the knot of despair slowly unfurl deep inside. She trusted Brody, knew with a certainty he'd protect her and Jamie with his last breath.

Tossing the throw onto the arm of the chair, she stood and walked over to Brody. "Okay, my pity party is over. I've already spent too much time running from Evan, and it stops now. What can I do?"

"First thing, get something to eat."

"Brody, I'm not—"

"We missed dinner. You need to eat, keep your strength up. If not for you, you need to be strong for your daughter." He clasped her hands gently between his. "Momma sent me in to get you. Dinner will be ready in five minutes. Just enough time for you to go check on Jamie and wash up."

She took a deep breath, then stood on her tiptoes and pressed a soft kiss against his cheek. "Thank you for being there for me."

"Always."

Brody stretched, feeling the ache in his low back from spending the night on the sofa. He'd refused to leave, wanting, no, *needing* to be close to Beth and Jamie. All the bedrooms were full up, Momma having called everybody home who could make it. Dane and Liam had doubled up. Lucas had showed up; he'd been down in San Antonio, researching a story, but had dropped everything the minute he'd heard there was trouble. Same thing with Ridge. Tessa shared her room with Serena.

Rafe had headed back into Shiloh Springs late last night, needing to be at the sheriff's office bright and early, to coordinate and assign shifts to make sure Beth and Jamie were watched round-the-clock, for as long as it took to capture Evan.

The scent of coffee hit first, followed almost immediately by the sweet, sweet scent of bacon. Rubbing a hand over his face, he grimaced at the stubble on his chin. Grabbing a shower was at the top of his list, but first he'd detour by the kitchen and grab a cup of coffee. He needed an infusion of caffeine to jumpstart his morning.

Before he'd taken more than a few steps, there was a knock on the front door. Scratching his stomach, he walked toward the door, a huge yawn causing his jaw to crack. Too many nights with too little sleep was starting to catch up with him.

"Greg?"

Greg Summers stood on the other side of the front door, a sheepish grin on his face. "Hey, Brody."

"Dude, what are you doing here?"

"I don't know. I stopped by your apartment, and when I couldn't find you there, this seemed like the next most obvious place." Greg gestured toward the door. "Mind if I come in?"

"Sorry. Just woke up. Long night." He motioned Greg inside, and pointed toward the kitchen. "I need coffee. Want some?"

Greg grinned. "I would love some."

Making their way to the kitchen, Brody stopped short at the sight of his mother and Tessa, doing a kind of choreographed dance around the kitchen. One worked the toaster, while the other scrambled eggs on the stove. A huge platter of crispy bacon sat on the countertop, and if he wasn't mistaken, Brody could swear he smelled his momma's homemade cinnamon rolls. His stomach growled, and Tessa smiled at him.

"Breakfast is almost ready." She spotted Greg standing

beside him, a faint blush staining her cheeks. "Oh, sorry, didn't know you had company. Y'all want some coffee?"

"Morning, Tessa. This is Greg Summers, and, yes, we'd love some coffee." He strode across the kitchen and dropped a kiss on his mother's cheek. "Good morning, Momma."

"You sleep okay, son?" Her sharp-eyed stare didn't miss a thing, he knew.

"I got some sleep. Momma, you remember Greg Summers?"

"Of course I do, I'm not senile yet." She nudged Brody aside, and hugged Greg. "How are your parents doing? I do miss spending time with your mother." With the familiarity only a mother could get away with, she cupped Greg's cheeks. "Is everything okay? You look tired."

"Everything's fine, Ms. Patti. My folks are doing good. Mom's getting the treatment she needs in Florida, and Dad's spoiling her rotten. I came up to talk to Brody about the fire. Thought I'd better drive up and see the damage for myself, maybe get some pictures to send to my dad. He's...upset about the barn going up in flames. He was counting on selling the property."

"If you can give me a couple of minutes to change, I'll take you over to look at the barn." Brody grabbed the cup of coffee Tessa held out, taking a long sip. "Thanks, Tessa."

"No hurry, Brody. I should probably have called first, but since it's the weekend, I figured I'd drive up, look at the damage, and answer any questions you might have."

"Appreciate it." He glanced toward his mother and Tessa, who'd moved back to the stove and toaster, continuing breakfast. "I do have a few questions. I'd planned on calling you the first part of the week once I had more answers, but since you're here..."

Greg held the mug Tessa had given him, staring down into it like it held the mystery of the universe in its dark depths. He shook his head before looking at Brody. "I can't wrap my head around the place burning down. Do you have any idea what happened?"

Brody gave a subtle shake of his head, letting Greg know he didn't want to answer. Not yet. He'd answer his questions once they were at the Summers' homestead, because he had some questions of his own, and he didn't want to ask them while he had an audience. Besides, Greg might feel more comfortable around their old stomping grounds.

Brody walked over to his mother and whispered low enough Greg couldn't hear. "I need to take him over to his family's place. I won't be gone long. Can you take care of Beth and Jamie? I'll give Rafe a call, make sure he knows I'll be gone for a little while."

"Beth will be fine. So will Jamie. Your brothers are here. Your father is here, too. Nobody's getting within a mile of either one of them, I promise."

"Thanks, Momma. Love you."

"Love you too. Now, git." She playfully swatted at him with the dish towel in her hand. "I got a whole passel of

123

hungry people to feed, and don't need you underfoot."

Grinning, he snagged a couple pieces of bacon, stuffing them in his mouth, and jogged out of the kitchen. Knowing Beth would be taken care of while he dealt with Greg made him feel easier about taking him over to the site of the fire. He had questions, and he hoped his suspicions were wrong.

He needed to wait, get the results from the lab in Austin. Concrete evidence what he suspected was, in fact, true. Within minutes, he was dressed and headed for the door. Greg joined him, and they climbed into Brody's truck and headed for the Summers' place.

The ride took about twenty minutes, and they caught up on the things happening in their lives. Greg had started a new job a couple of months earlier, and was dating a woman he'd met at his previous job. From the way his voice warmed when he talked about her, he obviously cared about her. He hoped Greg found some happiness, because he knew things would change as his parents aged, and his mother's cancer worsened.

Following the dirt and gravel road turnoff toward the barn, Brody gave a curse and sped up until he was parallel with the barn. The brakes squealed as the truck rocketed to a halt, and Brody slammed his fist against the steering wheel.

Smoke spiraled upward from the charred remains of the barn. The walls, which had remained from the initial fire, now lay in ashes and ruin, the stench of gasoline and smoke choking the air.

"What's going on?" Horror colored Greg's voice.

"Looks like once wasn't enough. The barn's been burned again."

CHAPTER TWELVE

Evan grumbled a curse, rolling over on the cold, bare concrete floor. Every bone, every joint ached as he scooted back to lean against the dirty, nasty, grease-stained wall. He'd managed to find an abandoned garage space away from town. It had taken far longer to reach the outskirts of Shiloh Springs than he'd planned. Turns out Shiloh Springs wasn't some little Podunk town in the middle of nowhere, it was also the name of the county, a lot of which was covered by nothing but dirt, trees, and a bunch of dead-looking bushes.

Getting this far had been a chore, one he hadn't anticipated. Turns out, most people in Texas were leery about picking up hitchhikers. Who'd have thought it? After all, Texans were supposed to be friendly, kind, and courteous to strangers. Ha, what a crock! Only two cars had stopped the entire time he'd been walking with his thumb out, and he'd ended up hoofing it most of the way.

When he wasn't hiding.

Every bone ached from lying on the hard, cold concrete. Of course, it was still better than sleeping outside. One more thing he could lay at Beth's feet. One more black mark she'd pay for when he caught up to her. Her ledger contained page after page of black tally marks, and he'd make sure she'd pay for each one.

Brushing off his wrinkled clothes as best he could in the diffused morning light spilling through the filthy windows, he stared at the pattern of sunlight sparkling on the broken glass sprinkled along the ground, projecting prisms of light against dirty, graffiti-stained walls.

"I can't believe I've sunk this low. Scrounging around dumps like this for a place to sleep. No food, no water. Not even a pot to piss in."

With a last frowning look around, he stepped outside, shielding his eyes with his hand, letting them adjust to the sudden change in lighting. Taking a deep breath, he stretched, loosening up his muscles. His mind whirled, thoughts bouncing around like bingo balls in one of those automated hoppers, while scene after scene of what he'd do when he caught up with Beth raced through his head. A crooked smile tugged at his lips with every image, each nastier than the one before.

He knew he couldn't simply walk up to her in the middle of town. There'd be far too many people around. Besides, she'd feel safe with her friends and family around her. Not to mention those blasted Boudreaus. Especially that scum-sucking sheriff and his equally pesky brother. He really wanted to meet Rafe Boudreau in a dark alley. Give him five minutes and he'd eliminate him, painfully and finally.

And Tessa. Oh, sweet little Tessa owed him big time. Most of the blame for his current dilemma lay directly at Tessa's door. If she'd given him the Crowley County bond, he'd be living the good life in another country, instead of having been sentenced to decades behind bars. And while he was at it, he might as well add his attorney to the list of people who needed to pay for betraying him. Camilla ended up finding somebody to take his case, because she felt horrible he was behind bars. She was sweet and naïve, totally gullible, and believed every word out of his mouth. Hook, line, and sinker.

And the idiot lawyer? More like a mouse who'd convinced him to take a plea bargain, promising he'd get a slap on the wrist. Oh, yeah, he needed to pay, too.

Scanning the horizon, there was nothing except trees tangled with brush and weeds as far as he could see. The night before, he'd walked until he was ready to drop before stumbling upon this abandoned garage space. The stench of oil and gasoline lingered in the air, stale yet pungent, even though it was apparent the place hadn't been used in years. But it had one advantage that made it perfect. It was close to Shiloh Springs, and that's what mattered. Too bad he didn't know how to hotwire a car, or he'd have made it here a heck of a lot sooner.

In the end, none of that mattered, though. Today was looking up. Soon he'd have everything he wanted.

Money.

Freedom.

But, more than either of those things, the one thing driving him forward was finally in his grasp—vengeance.

Beth made her way to the kitchen after her shower. Her hair was still damp, and she'd borrowed a set of clothes from Nica, not wanting to put on the clothes from the night before. She absently ran a comb through it, working out the tangles as she walked down the steps, following the scent of fresh-brewed coffee like it was a siren's song. Which in all honesty, it was. She'd didn't function well without at least two full cups every morning.

"Good morning, Beth. Did you get any sleep at all?" Ms. Patti leaned against the countertop by the stove, a mug of coffee in her hand, which she passed to Beth. She inhaled deeply before taking the first sip, closing her eyes as the warmth from the liquid nirvana flooded her senses. How was it possible Ms. Patti was not only the best cook she knew, but apparently also was the queen of caffeine?

"I managed to get a couple hours. I kept jerking awake at every sound. Has there been any news? Have they caught Evan?"

"Not yet, hon. Rafe's at the sheriff's station, got there early. I talked to him a couple hours ago. Everyone is looking for Evan. He can't hide for long."

"I'm sorry I brought all my problems to your doorstep."

"Nonsense." Ms. Patti slapped two pieces of toast onto a plate loaded with scrambled eggs and bacon. "You haven't done anything wrong. Evan gets all the blame here, so you stop that line of thinking right now." She motioned Beth to the table, and plopped the plate in front of her when she sat.

"My head tells me that, Ms. Patti. Except, none of you would be dealing with him if he wasn't obsessed with me. Or rather, the money he thinks I have. Why can't he understand? I couldn't keep the money. After everything he and Trevor did, it was dirty—blood money."

Ms. Patti lowered into the chair across from Beth. "Honey, you did nothing wrong. Nothing. Neither did your sister. I've gotten to know you both in the last few months. You'd never have kept that money anyway. Tell me honestly, if you'd know the Crowley County Bond wasn't simply a family keepsake, but was in fact worth a lot of money, what would you have done?"

Beth took another sip of her coffee, savoring the sweetness before answering. "We'd have done exactly what we did, donate it back to Crowley County."

"Precisely." Ms. Patti reached across and squeezed her hand.

"I checked in on Jamie before my shower. She was sleeping, and I didn't want to wake her. I don't know what or even how much I should be telling her. She's so little, I'm not even sure she comprehends why we're not living with her daddy, and why he isn't around anymore."

"It's a tough situation to be in, hon. Not something most people have to deal with telling their children. My guess is to play it by ear. If she asks questions, explain it in the simplest, easiest way you can, but until then, it might be better to let her be surrounded by people who love her."

Beth set the coffee mug on the tabletop, wrapping her hands around it to ward off the sudden chill sweeping through her. "I can't imagine Evan ever hurting Jamie. Me, I can take care of myself, but she's so little." She heard the crack in her voice, and paused, working on gaining a modicum of composure. "Ms. Patti, I'm terrified he's going to take my baby to hurt me."

"Not going to happen. Brody, Rafe, all of us aren't going to allow Evan within a mile of you or your daughter. I give you my word, he's going to get caught." Ms. Patti gave her a steely-eyed glare, and stood up, her bearing intimidating for all her tiny stature. "I've got the right to protect myself and my property. That applies to anybody within these walls. If he steps foot on Boudreau land, I'd consider that a threat."

"Ms. Patti, you can't—"

"Trust me, I can. I've taken out any number of varmints on my property, and shooting troublemakers intent on doing harm to me and mine, I've got no problem taking out another one. Besides," she grinned, her expression deliciously wicked, "I've got a brand-new shotgun I've been itching to try out."

Before Beth could think of anything to say, she heard the clump of running feet down the stairs, right before Jamie sprinted into the kitchen, her hair pulled up into two ponytails, a small pair of bib overalls with a bright yellow T-shirt underneath. Nica trailed close behind, wiping her eyes. Beth winced at the obvious dark circles under her friend's eyes. She'd obviously taken her job as guard dog seriously. Catching Beth's eyes, she winked and headed for the coffee maker.

"Good morning, Mommy!" Jamie threw herself into Beth's embrace, smacking a kiss against her cheek. "Guess what? Nica gave me these clothes. Aren't they something? She said they was hers when she was little, like me."

"She's right, Jamie." Ms. Patti placed a glass of juice beside Beth's coffee mug. "Nica did wear those when she was younger. She griped and complained forever because she wanted a pair like her big brother Dane wore when he worked with the horses." Ms. Patti winked at her daughter, who simply rolled her eyes and sipped her coffee.

"Can I go see the horses?" Jamie turned a pleading glance her way, and Beth's heart melted.

"Breakfast first, then maybe."

"Yay, horses!" Jamie sat in the chair beside Beth's and reached for the juice, taking a big swallow. Beth loved seeing the excitement and joy filling her daughter. It was funny how kids rebounded from just about everything that got thrown their way. Jamie had adjusted amazingly well to her father's defection, moving halfway across the country, and even changing schools.

School! She'd have to let Mrs. Gleason know Jamie wouldn't be in attendance for a couple of days at least.

Nica plopped into the chair across from Beth. "You get any sleep?"

"A little. Thank you for staying with Jamie."

"No problem, she's a sweetheart."

"You hear that, Mommy. I'm a sweetheart!" Jamie grinned and a tiny trickle of juice slid down her chin.

"You are indeed, cutie pie. How about some toast, would you like that?"

"Can I have—"

"Nope, no waffles. Today, you get toast with butter and honey."

Jamie perked up at the word honey. She loved honey and if she had her way, it'd be slathered on everything she ate. It was one concession Beth allowed, because it was natural sugar, something she could control, rather than something loaded with all kinds of junk. Not that she'd been super-strict about Jamie's diet lately, but she was happy her child wasn't a finicky eater.

Beth started to rise, and Ms. Patti motioned her back in her seat. With ease of long practice, she popped two slices of bread into the toaster, and pulled a bottle of honey from the cupboard. Within minutes, Jamie was chowing down on her toast.

"Can you keep an eye on Jamie for a couple of minutes? I need to call Mrs. Gleason, let her know Jamie won't be in for a day or two."

"Good idea," Ms. Patti gestured Beth toward the door. "We've got this."

Pulling her cell phone from her pocket, Beth quickly apprised the kindergarten teacher about Jamie's absence, the other woman understanding and offering help. It was one more reason she'd fallen in love with Shiloh Springs. They'd been welcomed with open arms from the moment they'd first visited, coming to stay with Tessa after the debacle with Evan. She'd been made to feel at home. It had been a major factor in her decision to relocate, second only to her sister living there.

Glancing through the window of the living room, she spotted Douglas and Dane talking, their expressions serious. As she watched the two men, noting how similar they appeared, right down to their stance, a motorcycle roar could be heard roaring up the drive leading to the house, a lone rider straddling the sleek chrome and black machine. A black helmet obscured his face from view, yet somehow Beth knew this was somebody she'd never met before. He pulled to a stop beside Douglas and Dane, letting the engine of the great beast purr at a low rumble before cutting the engine. Straightening to his full height, he alighted and strode over to the two men, throwing his arms around Douglas in what could only be described as a bear hug, which he returned with a couple of thumps on the stranger's back.

Stepping back, he tugged the helmet off, revealing dark blond hair that easily brushed the collar of his black leather jacket. Taller than either man he stood with, he had to top close to six and a half feet, broad shoulders encased in black leather. Even through the window, air of danger surrounded him. He looked familiar. Somewhere she'd seen him before, and from the way Douglas greeted him, he was either a member of the family or somebody close.

While Douglas and Dane headed toward the barn, the stranger strode toward the front door, his legs eating up the distance in long strides. There was a predatory grace in his walk, a controlled element of danger that sent a shiver down Beth's spine. She didn't want to get on the wrong side of this man.

"Momma?" The word accompanied the opening of the front door, and Beth heard a sharp gasp from the kitchen before Ms. Patti came barreling into the hall.

"Heath? Oh, my stars, Heath!"

The tall man lifted Ms. Patti off the floor like she weighed nothing, spinning around in a circle, a huge grin on his face. "I've missed you. What's for supper?"

Ms. Patti swatted him on the chest. "Put me down. I can't believe the first words out of your mouth are about food. Everybody else is eating breakfast, and you're asking about supper." She shook her head slowly, but Beth spotted her amused expression.

"I have been dreaming about your chicken fried steak for the last fifteen hundred miles. East coast food just doesn't taste as good as yours, Momma." The distinct whine in his voice disappeared when he spotted Beth. "Sorry, I didn't know you had company."

Ms. Patti practically dragged him over to Beth. "Heath, this is Beth Stewart. Beth, this is my son, Heath. I'm not sure what he's doing here, since he lives in Virginia." Her eyes studied her son intently. "But I'm sure he's gonna tell me—soon."

"Hello, Beth. Pleasure to meet you." Beth stood still beneath his perusal, knowing he sized her up, as she did him.

"Mommy, can I see the horses now?" Jamie's full-speed dash skidded to a half and she shrank back at the edge of the hall when she spotted Heath, her expression wary.

"Jamie, this is Heath, Ms. Patti's son. He's come to visit with her and Mr. Douglas." Beth slid her arm around Jamie's shoulder, pulling her against her side. Jamie stared up at the tall man, a mixture of trepidation and excitement flooding her expression.

"Hello." She looked up at Beth. "Am I supposed to call him Uncle Heath or Mr. Heath?"

Heath squatted down, bringing him closer down to Jamie's level, his smile filled with kindness and warmth. "Hi, Jamie. It's very nice to meet you. If you're a friend of my momma, I'd like it if you called me Uncle Heath." He held out his hand, and Jamie reached forward, her smaller one engulfed in his outstretched one. Looking up at Beth, he winked, and Jamie knew he had to be a hit with the ladies. He seemed a natural-born flirt.

Nica popped out of the kitchen, and nodded once to Beth, blew a smacking kiss to her brother, and Jamie followed her like a trained puppy. "Come on, pipsqueak, I'll go to the barn with you."

"Come back to the kitchen and I'll fix you some breakfast. I'll need to take down some steaks, too, since it looks like I'm making chicken fried steak for supper." Without waiting, Ms. Patti breezed past them, Beth and Heath following meekly in her wake.

Beth refilled her mug, and got one for Heath too, figuring he could doctor it the way he liked it. He wrapped his hands around the mug, and studied her intently, a look of quiet speculation evident, which was quickly masked behind a cheeky grin.

"What's your story, pretty Beth? What brings you to the Boudreau house?"

"I'll fill you in later, Heath," Ms. Patti interrupted, slapping a huge plate of bacon, scrambled eggs, and toast in front of him. "And stop flirting with her, she's taken."

Heath quirked a brow at her words, and Beth felt a wash of heat flood her face.

"Taken, is she? Too bad." He glanced at Ms. Patti. "Who?"

"Brody."

"Ah."

Beth watched the back and forth, her eyes widening at Ms. Patti's declaration. *I'm taken? News to me.*

"I think I'll go check on Jamie." She headed for the back door like hellhounds had sprouted up through the kitchen floor, and half jogged, half walked toward the barn. Whew, that had been intense. But the more she thought about it, the more she realized she'd overreacted to Heath's arrival. He wasn't the enemy. He wasn't a threat to her daughter. The man had every right to be at the Boudreau homestead. It was his home, although if she remembered right, he lived in Virginia and worked in D.C. One of those government agencies with abbreviations, though she couldn't remember which one.

On reaching the barn, she took a deep breath, and pasted an excited expression on her face, ready to face her daughter and put on a happy front. Ms. Patti's words ran through her head. They thought she belonged with Brody?

Would it really be so bad to be loved by someone like Brody? He was caring, sweet. He loved her daughter. Without a doubt, he's nothing like Evan.

Somehow, the thought of being with Brody didn't scare her, didn't make her want to run screaming for the hills in the opposite direction. In fact, if she got the chance, she'd run toward him.

This is crazy. We haven't even been on a single date. Yet I can't stop thinking about him, wanting to be near him. It can't be wrong to feel this way. Oh, who am I kidding, we haven't even kissed.

A bubble of excitement flitted through her, and she felt giddy. A flicker of hope raced through her, and she grasped it with both hands. No more running. No more hiding. No more refusing to live her life on her terms. Once she'd been a strong independent woman, capable of making her own decisions and running her life on her terms. Somehow over the years, she allowed Evan to turn her into a different person.

Never again. Starting today, she was taking back her life. Grabbing hold with both hands to what she wanted, and never letting go.

And what she wanted was Brody Boudreau.

CHAPTER THIRTEEN

B rody climbed out of the cab of the pickup and sprinted toward the smoldering ruins of the Summers' barn. Plumes of white smoke spiraled upward from the charred remains, and he kicked at a clump of dirt, needing an outlet for his frustration and anger, but unwilling to show any emotion while Greg stood mere feet away.

"What happened?"

"I wish I knew. When I came by here yesterday, nothing had changed. Most of the barn burned, but some portions of the walls still stood. Now, here," he pointed to a new pattern of burn wear, "there's evidence of accelerant use. Here and here."

"Wait...wait! Are you telling me somebody burned this down a second time? I don't understand. Are you saying this is arson? Why? Who? This doesn't make any sense." Greg started forward, and Brody grasped his arm, stopping him in his tracks.

"You can't go in there, Greg. It's too dangerous. Besides, this is an active crime scene."

"Crime scene?" Shock laced Greg's words, and all the

color leeched from his face.

"I wasn't going to say anything yet, not until we have definitive proof from the lab in Austin, but, yes, we suspect arson." He watched Greg closely, trying to gauge his reaction. He didn't suspect his friend, but then again, he couldn't automatically discount him. Hadn't he shown up only hours after the barn had been torched again? Somebody was attempting to cover up their crime. Too bad he'd already collected all the samples and evidence and delivered it to the Arson Laboratory's investigative teams in Austin.

"Why? There's nothing here but an abandoned, run-down barn and the house." He turned abruptly and took off running toward the farmhouse, Brody on his heels. He caught up within a few yards, and pulled Greg to a stop, keeping him from getting any closer to his old family home. With this second attempt at burning the barn, the entire Summers' property was now considered an active scene, and he couldn't let Greg get any closer to contaminate any evidence.

"Stop, Greg. I need to call this in. I'm sorry, but you can't go in there."

Greg's head hung low, shoulders slumped. "I don't understand, Brody. Who would do this?"

"That's what I'm going to find out. But you can't be here, Greg. I'm going to call one of my brothers, get you a ride. I'll need to ask you some questions, go over what we know thus far."

"Okay. Do what you need to do, find out who did this. Why they did this." He paused and stared into the distance, and Brody wondered what he saw. It had to be hard; this was Greg's childhood home. "I need to call Dad."

"I'll handle it. I'm going to have them take you to the sheriff's office, where we can talk without interruptions, okay?"

"Whatever." Greg shook his head, staring at the charred remains of his family's barn. "I can't believe this. I've wracked my brain trying to figure out why somebody burned the barn down in the first place. I figured maybe it was teens messing around, you know? Hiding out from their parents like we did when we were kids. Smoking a little pot. Maybe sneaking out here to meet their girlfriends. But this? I don't get it."

"We'll figure it out, Greg. Now give me a second, and I'll call someone for that ride."

It didn't take long before he got hold of Chance. Since it was the weekend, his brother wasn't in court, and agreed to pick Greg up and stay with him at Rafe's office until Brody could get there. Within fifteen minutes, Greg was handled, and Brody called the fire station, and had Jeff Barnes meet him at the Summers' barn.

"Tell me what you see."

Jeff wrapped his hands in gloves and pointed toward the burned rubble. "Looks like accelerant use here and here." He delineated the pattern Brody spotted earlier, confirming his suspicions. "New marks attempting to obscure the old burn pattern." His eyes met Brody's. "Somebody trying to cover their tracks maybe?"

"That's my thinking."

Jeff shook his head. "What's so important about this place it merits not one, but two blazes? There's something I'm not seeing here."

"I haven't wrapped my head around that yet. But adding it to the two previous fires, and we've got a pattern emerging. One I don't like."

"Me either, boss. You hear anything back from the lab yet?"

Brody shook his head. "I put a rush on it, and left another message on their machine. Hoping they'll call back before I question Greg."

"Greg? Greg Summers? What's he doing in Shiloh Springs?"

"He showed up this morning, wanting to see the place. That's how we found out about the second burn."

"Gotcha. Guess it makes sense, seeing his family's owned the property for decades. Bit of a coincidence though, him showing up without calling."

"Maybe. Can't read too much into it, since his parents live in Florida now, and it would be difficult for them to come back to Texas. San Antonio's not far, couple hours' drive. It's what I'd do, if it was me."

"I guess." Jeff walked gingerly between the fallen debris,

careful with each step not to disturb any evidence. Brody continued to be amazed at how far Jeff had progressed during his time with the fire station. Former military brat, he'd moved to Shiloh Springs a few years previous. He'd joined the fire department after six months or so. His father was a friend of Douglas', having served together in the Army.

"Gimme your gut instinct. Why this place? What makes it different than the other fires?"

"Similarities, all abandoned properties. Hadn't been lived in for several years. Out of the way locations for the most part, not on main roads or highways. No witnesses. But this one? It seems more—personal—for lack of a better word. I'm thinking gasoline for the accelerant, because that'd be easy to obtain. Whoever did this didn't want anything left of the old place. Since the first fire didn't destroy everything, they came back to finish the job. But, and here's my question. Was it to destroy every square inch of the place, make it disappear for whatever personal reason the fire starter had? Or was this second fire done to try and cover up any trace and contaminate the findings of the first fire?"

Brody shrugged, because he'd had the same questions, even if his gut was telling him it wasn't an either/or question, more a how much of each reason contributed to the second blaze. They finished gathering up, packaging, and labeling evidence they could, and took numerous photos of the scene. Brody knew they'd be useful in comparing them to the first set of pics.

"Can you load everything on the floor of my truck? I need to make some calls, see if I can gain some insight into this second attempt to destroy the site." He wished he could catch a break, because he needed to catch this firebug before he set any more fires. Last thing Shiloh Springs needed was to get the citizenry up in arms about a serial arsonist roaming their streets.

"Sure thing, boss."

Pulling out his phone, he started to call Ben Summers, but stopped before he hit dial. Instead, he tapped the speed-dial for Beth.

"Good morning, Brody."

"Did you get any sleep? How're you doing this morning?"

Beth chuckled and the sound did funny things to his insides. "Yes, I got some sleep, and I'm fine. Jamie's gone out to the barn with Nica to see the horses, and I'm sitting here talking to your mother."

"She'll take good care of you. Bet she's already stuffed you full of breakfast and asked what you want for lunch."

"Absolutely. Did *you* get any sleep?" The emphasis on you made him smile.

"I got enough. Sorry I didn't get to see you this morning, but I had to head with an old friend to look at his property."

"The one you've been worrying about? And don't tell me you haven't been worrying, because I can tell when you're thinking about your job."

"Paid that much attention to me, have you?" At her indignant squawk, he rushed on. "You're right. There's been some stuff going on at work, and it's kept me preoccupied, though not too much I haven't thought about you. Speaking of, I'm sorry our date got derailed. Just so you know, this is only a postponement, and not a cancellation. You're not getting out of taking me to dinner that easily."

He loved the sound of her laughter. Hearing it brightened any day, no matter how glum, and now was no exception. Jeff walked by with the evidence bags, heading for Brody's truck, and he knew he had to cut things short. Work called, and in his line of work that meant twenty-four seven. Didn't matter it was a Saturday morning, fires burned without respect to scheduled days off.

"Oh, I should probably tell you, I met your brother this morning."

"Which one?"

"Heath."

He could practically hear the smile in her voice, and he bit back a possessive growl. "Didn't know he was in town."

"He showed up this morning. He's quite—something—isn't he?"

"Don't fall for anything he says, Beth. Heath is the biggest flirt you'll ever meet. I love my brother, but he's definitely a ladies' man."

"Oh, I figured that out pretty quick. And your mother set him straight."

Uh, oh. Heath must have been flirting up a storm if Momma stepped in. He smiled, picturing his diminutive mother standing up to the walking mountain and shaking her finger under his nose. She'd have to get a stepstool if she really wanted to get in Heath's face, but she'd have no problem doing exactly that. Wouldn't be the first time, and definitely wouldn't be the last.

"Did she now? Anything I need to know about?"

She hesitated before answering. "Not really." The way she answered piqued his curiosity more than the actual words, but he didn't have time to get into it now. But definitely later...

"Listen, I've gotta run. I just wanted to hear your voice, let you brighten my day. I'll see you later, okay?"

"Yes. Stay safe, Brody."

"I will. Talk to you soon."

He hung up before he could make a bigger fool of himself. Those three little words wanted to spring to his lips, but with her ex on the loose, this would be the worst time to tell her how he felt. But soon, he promised himself, he let her know in word and deed exactly how he felt about her. He prayed it would be soon, because he was tired of putting his life on hold, keeping his feelings in check, instead of being with the woman he loved.

But for now—he had an arsonist to catch.

CHAPTER FOURTEEN

Brody strode through the door of the sheriff's station with more questions than he'd started the morning with. After Greg left, he'd called Ben Summers, and spent an inordinate amount of time explaining what happened and asking him pointed questions, ones he'd rather not have had to ask. Ben had broken down sobbing when Brody explained about the second fire. During their call, Ben admitted Sandra's cancer had returned, and the treatments the specialists recommended were both painful and expensive. Brody didn't have the heart to tell Ben he couldn't sell the property, not until the investigation was completed. Ben offered to fly back to Texas, but Brody assured him he'd handle everything he could remotely, and Ben and Sandra wouldn't have to come back, not unless they turned up something to change the status of the case.

"Can I get you some coffee, Brody?" Sally Anne jumped up from behind her desk, and gave him a quick hug. Sally Anne was a fixture at the Shiloh Springs sheriff's office, a middle-aged dynamo who worked there as a sort of Jill-of-All-Trades. Brody didn't care it might not be considered professional; he'd known Sally Anne most of his life. If she wanted to give him a hug, let her hug away. He considered her family, and he didn't stand on formality with family.

"No thanks, Sally Anne. Chance and Greg Summers in the back?"

"Yeah. Rafe got called to deal with that McAllister boy again. Said he'd be back as soon as he can." Leaning in, she whispered, "His mother sounded real upset, almost like she was crying in the background." Ah, there was the Sally Anne he knew and loved. She was a sweetheart, but she loved spreading a little bit of gossip. Never intentionally to hurt someone, that wasn't who she was, but load her up with a juicy tidbit here and there, and she was a happy camper.

"Gotcha."

He pulled off his cowboy hat and slapped it against his thigh as he walked down the long hall, ending up at the conference room. This room had been a hotbed of activity over the last few months, more than it usually saw in a year. Like most small towns, Shiloh Springs had the occasional criminal activity, but nothing anybody would call major. Some weeks the biggest story might be Eliza and Dennis Boatwright sampling too much of their home brew, and getting a little loud and rowdy. Brody had lost count of the number of times Rafe made house calls on the local couple. They'd never intentionally hurt anybody, but they liked a bit of a tipple more than a bit. Brewing their own beer wasn't illegal, though Brody got the impression they might brew more than beer, but he couldn't prove it. As long as nobody got hurt, live and let live.

Opening the door to the conference room, he spotted Chance leaning back in his chair, hands folded across his midsection, seated across from Greg. Greg had regained the color in his face, but still looked kinda lost.

"Greg, I talked to your dad. Updated him on everything. He wanted to fly here, but I told him to stay with your mom."

Greg shifted in his chair, and ran a hand through his hair, mussing it even more. "Good. The last thing he needs is more stress right now. Did he tell you about mom's new treatments?"

Brody slid into one of the chairs lining the long table, and tossed his hat on the one beside him. "Yeah. I'm sorry to hear about her cancer returning."

"I hate it. It's a horrible, painful way to live. We'd hoped with the last round of chemo it was gone for good. She was doing really well. Her and Dad were doing things again, going out and having fun. Now, it's like she's fallen into a deep, dark hole she can't climb out of. And the treatments, they're worse than the disease."

"I'm sorry. Is there anything they need?" Chance's voice was filled with compassion.

Greg shook his head again. "Everything that can be done is being done. I know Dad's been hoping to sell the property, to help offset the costs of the new treatments. Now, with this setback…" His voice trailed off and he leaned back in the chair, and scrubbed his hands across his face.

"We'll get it figured out as soon as we can, I promise. I'll talk to Momma, see what we can do about getting the place sold once the case is cleared. Hang in there, Greg."

"Unless you need me for anything, I've gotta head out." Chance stood and shook Greg's hand. "Hang in there. Brody will figure out who burned your property, and I'll be more than happy to prosecute them."

"I've got it covered. Thanks, bro."

After Chance left, Brody looked at Greg, wishing he really didn't have to question his friend, but what choice did he have? There weren't any suspects. Maybe with a little judicious prodding, Greg might be able to come up with some info, some subconscious knowledge that might click with a little poking beneath the surface.

"Go ahead, Brody. Ask me whatever you need to know."

"Can you think of anybody who'd want to set the fire, intentionally or otherwise?"

"No. I mean, who'd have a reason for setting an abandoned, dilapidated, half-falling-down structure on fire? I have thought about it, wracked my brain, asking that question over and over, and I can't come up with a single name."

"Okay. When I asked your dad, he said he hadn't kept up the insurance payments to cover the home or the barn, thinking it would sell right away. Did you know that?"

"I knew. Brody, I've gotta tell you something, and it's gonna make me look guilty as sin. When Dad told me what he was going to do, let the policies lapse because they didn't have the money with Mom's treatments, I couldn't let it go. The place, barn and house, it's still insured. I made arrangements with the insurance company, took over the payments on the policy. I didn't tell him or Mom. You know how he is: his stubborn pride wouldn't have let me keep making the payments. So I kept it to myself."

"Neither of your parents know about you keeping up the payments?"

Greg stood, pushing his chair all the way back against the wall, his movements awkward and stiff. "I've kept making those payments for the last couple of years, ever since they moved to Florida. We expected the property to sell right away, but when it didn't, I couldn't bring myself to stop paying for the insurance. Just because I didn't want to live there, didn't mean it wasn't worth something. It's a prime piece of real estate, and I'm really surprised it hasn't sold. Also, I figured if a buyer knew the place was insured, it might be more appealing toward a sale."

"How much is the place insured for?"

"Whatever amount Dad had on there. I didn't change it or raise it, I simply continued making the payments." He stopped pacing, and closed his eyes, concentrating hard. "If I remember right, I think the whole place is covered for about a million and a quarter."

Brody jotted down the figure, next to his notes about Greg making the payments. This was another angle he'd have to look into, because it put a different spin on motive. He got a little tingle on the back of his neck, the one he got whenever his instincts started kicking it, and figured he might be onto something. Money made people do crazy things.

"Wasn't it hard to keep up those payments, Greg? Insurance, especially that amount, isn't cheap."

Greg ran a hand through his hair, leaving it sticking up on top like a rooster's coxcomb. "I guess. Never really thought about it. They'd send the bill and I'd pay it all in one lump sum. Took it out of savings and didn't worry about it until the next year, when it came due." His body stiffened and he stared at Brody, his face a mask of horror. "You don't think I did this? Brody, that farm was my home. My father's place. His father's before him."

"I'm not accusing you of anything. Calm down. I have to cover all my bases. Insurance fraud is huge. You'd be surprised how many people think they can get away with burning down their place, covering it with huge insurance policies. But that's only one angle here, and easily disproven. It won't take long to rule out money as a motive."

"Good. I'm still trying to wrap my head around somebody burning down the barn. I know it wasn't much to look at, but it had been standing for decades. Like the house. It doesn't make sense. Do you think maybe kids did it? You know, a dare or something?"

"Right now, I'm looking into anything and everything. I won't stop until I know how it happened and who did it." Brody's voice came out harsher than he intended, and he watched the color drain from Greg's face. He plopped back into the chair he'd vacated earlier, looking like the weight of the world pressed down on him and he was suffocating under the pressure.

"You okay?"

Gregg shook himself, his whole body jerking. "Yeah. We about done here? This has all been a bit much—I guess it affected me more than I thought it would. I need to head home, unless you've got more questions?"

"That'll do for now, Greg. If I need anything else, I'll give you a call."

Brody watched Greg slowly rise from the chair and start down the hall. He turned back once, and gave a half-hearted wave, and then disappeared out the front door. With a sigh, he followed, knowing Greg had forgotten his car was still at the Big House. Shock would do that to a person.

With a quick wave to Sally Anne, he caught up with Greg standing on the sidewalk, and drove him back to his family's ranch, then watched him head back to San Antonio. That little niggle of instinct told him there was something else, something more, behind the Summers' fire, and he was close. Facts and figures raced through his head, spinning and swirling, beginning to coalesce into a picture—one he hoped was wrong. Because if his instincts were on point, more than one family would suffer as a result.

Sometimes he really hated being right.

CHAPTER FIFTEEN

B eth stood on the front porch, and watched the white sedan driving toward the Big House. Camilla called from Houston earlier, after picking up her rental car, letting Beth know she was on her way. Camilla had been crying, anxious and upset about Evan's escape. She'd gotten a call from the FBI, questioning her about her brother's whereabouts and warning her to contact them if her brother contacted her in any way. Beth couldn't imagine Evan contacting Camilla, not after Camilla cut ties with him after he took the plea deal.

Stepping off the porch, Beth waited for her to park the car beside Ms. Patti's white Escalade before walking to meet her. Camilla threw herself into Beth's arms, her red eyes indicating Beth was right about her tears.

"I'm sorry!"

"It's not your fault. Come on, let's go inside. Pop the trunk and I'll grab your bag."

"I can get it. It's just the one suitcase, since I won't be here long." Camilla lifted out the suitcase and slammed the trunk shut, before placing both hands on it and leaning forward. "How did things get so screwed up, Beth?"

"I've wondered that too. Looking back, I should have seen the signs Evan wasn't happy. I wasn't happy either, though I didn't want to admit it."

They walked into the house, and Camilla set her suitcase against the wall. "This place is gorgeous. I'll admit, I stopped at the end of the drive and stared at it for several minutes. It's like a combination of epic grandeur and a big warm welcome home."

"Wait until you meet the Boudreau family. You'll really understand that warm welcome part." Beth smiled at her friend. It didn't matter she was her former sister-in-law. It didn't matter Evan turned out to be a monster, intent on ruining her life. What mattered was the friendship she'd forged with Camilla from the day they'd met. Somehow, she needed to fight past Camilla's guilt, and get her to realize Beth didn't blame her for her brother's actions.

Beth led her into the kitchen, which was empty of people after a morning rush of Boudreaus traipsing in and out, grabbing breakfast and a quick chat. Ms. Patti had finally headed to her home office, intent on telecommuting this morning, and dealing with the gigantic mountain of paperwork, as she'd called it. Not that Beth believed it for a second. Ms. Patti was one of the most organized people she'd ever met. She ran her business and her family with an iron hand wrapped in a velvet glove, strict and firm yet with a dose of love. No doubt her home office was as organized as the one in town. The woman ran the biggest real estate office in Shiloh Springs and the surrounding counties, and not a day went by she didn't have her finger on the pulse of the buying and selling community. To say nothing of the woman knowing everything that went on in her town. And Beth meant *everything*.

"Where's Jamie?" Camilla laid her purse on the table, and looked around the kitchen. "I really need to catch up on my hugs."

Beth smiled. "She's in the barn. Last time I checked, she'd helped brush down the horses. Now she's playing with the kittens. One of the barn cats had a litter a couple of weeks ago. I'm praying she doesn't want to take one home with her when we leave."

There was an awkward silence for a few minutes after her statement, before Camilla touched Beth's arm. "We might as well talk about the five-hundred-pound elephant in the room and get it out of the way. What have the police said about Evan? Do they have any leads on where he is?"

Beth motioned for her to sit, and then pulled two glasses out of the cabinet, filling them with ice. She added sweet tea to both and handed one to Camilla before sitting at the table. She measured her words carefully; after all, good, bad, or indifferent, Camilla was still Evan's sister.

"Rafe, Tessa's fiancé, who's also the sheriff, is in constant contact with the officials at the prison, the Texas Highway Patrol, the Texas Rangers, the Austin FBI office, and a host of others looking into Evan's escape. Law enforcement throughout the state is looking for him."

"This is crazy. I keep wondering what he's thinking. Doesn't he know this can't end well?"

And isn't that the understatement of the year?

"I can't even presume to understand what's going on in Evan's head. I do know his cellmate was recaptured sometime during the night. Rafe heard about it early this morning. Axel Fleming, that's Evan's cellmate, and his girlfriend were arrested at the border, attempting to get into Mexico. Both claim they haven't seen Evan since they left him at a gas station. Tracks with the information we were given yesterday. Evan was last seen at one of those convenience store places, where he changed clothes and disappeared. One of the workers there reported to a state trooper somebody matching Evan's description came in and bought a bunch of snacks, water, and a map."

Beth toyed with the glass, tracing her finger along the lines of condensation. Her stomach still felt tied into knots every time she thought about Evan, out there who knows where. With every fiber of her being, she wished and prayed he was far, far away, and nowhere near Shiloh Springs. But the logical part of her, the part that knew how her ex thought—screamed he was headed toward Shiloh Springs— if he wasn't here already.

"A map? To where?"

"That's a good question. I don't think anybody mentioned it."

Before she could say more, the back door swung open and Jamie raced through, pigtails flying. "Mommy, the mommy kitty let me play with her babies—Aunt Milla!"

Beth laughed as Jamie threw herself into Camilla's lap, wrapping her arms around her aunt's neck in a near stranglehold. "Guess she missed you."

"Not as much as I've missed her. It is so good to see you, sweetie!"

Jamie giggled. "Everybody has funny names for me here. You call me sweetie. Uncle Brody calls me Honey Bear! I like that one, because I love honey. Mommy gave me butter and honey toast this morning."

Camilla's tear-filled eyes met Beth's over the top of Jamie's head, and she mouthed the words "thank you."

Beth gave her a wink, and picked up her tea, taking a sip. Never once had she doubted Camilla's love for Jamie, and Jamie adored her aunt. It felt right to let Camilla spend time with Jamie. None of the fiasco she called her life was Camilla's fault, and she refused to blame the other woman for the actions of another.

Glancing toward the open kitchen doorway, she spotted Nica standing on the porch, cautiously watching Beth and Jamie. She motioned for Nica to come in, but she shook her head, jerking her thumb over her shoulder toward the yard. Mouthing the words "I'll be back," she stepped off the porch, leaving the door ajar.

"Mommy, can I show Aunt Milla the baby kitties?"

Camilla's hand smoothed over the top of Jamie's head, tucking a loose wisp of hair behind her ear. "You have baby kittens? I love kittens. Are they pretty?"

Jamie nodded her head vigorously. "And soft. Ms. Patti and Mr. Douglas also got horses, and dogs, and chickens, and cows. The kind with horns. Uncle Dane let me pet one of the baby cows. Oh, and they got a donkey! His name's Otto."

"Otto? That's a funny name for a donkey."

"He's called Otto, a nickname for 'he ought to know better'." Ms. Patti walked in from the hall, a crooked smile coloring her words. Her affection for the critter was obvious from her playful tone. "That darned donkey gets into more trouble because he knows not to do some of the things he does, and yet he mule-headedly does them anyway."

"Camilla, this is Patricia Boudreau, the matriarch of the Boudreau clan. Ms. Patti, this is my friend, Camilla Stewart."

"Welcome to Shiloh Springs, Ms. Stewart."

"Thank you, Mrs. Boudreau. I've missed seeing Beth and this little munchkin." Her fingers dug into Jamie's sides, and she howled with laughter, squirming to get away from Camilla's teasing.

"How long will you be staying in Texas?"

"Well, I had only planned a day or two. I was bringing some papers the attorneys needed Evan to sign. I offered to bring them, thinking to kill two birds with one stone—make sure my brother signed everything, instead of stalling again, and getting to see Beth and this little troublemaker."

Ms. Patti smiled at Jamie's squeak of protest. "I happen to like troublemakers. They make the best kind of friends."

"Jamie, why don't you go and wash up? Make sure you scrub your hands and face really well."

"Okay, Mommy." She swiveled around on Camilla's lap. "You'll be here when I come back, right?"

"I'll be here." She made a cross symbol over her heart. "I promise."

Jamie held out her hand, her tiny fingers curled. "Pinky swear?"

Camilla chuckled, and looped her little finger with Jamie's. "Pinky swear."

Without another word, Jamie scrambled off her aunt's lap and raced toward the stairs, all three women watching her go.

"I don't know how you have the energy to keep up with the whirlwind. I'm exhausted and I've only been here five minutes." Camilla took a long drink of her tea.

"Jamie only seems to have one speed, and it's full throttle. She loves the yard at Tessa's cottage, our new place. Lots of space to run around and play. A big backyard, lots of grass. I haven't had a chance to meet the neighbors yet, but Tessa said they're all friendly and they'll keep an extra lookout for Jamie."

"From what little I could see driving through town, it seems charming. I'd love to explore it, if I have the time." Camilla stood, smoothing down the ruffled cotton maxi-style skirt she wore. "Speaking of which, can you recommend a hotel or motel, some place to stay while I'm here?"

Beth sucked in a breath of surprise. "Oh, no! Within everything going on with Evan, I totally forgot you were staying with me—us."

"It's okay, Beth. You didn't plan on having your world turned upside-down by my brother again, and having to leave your home. I'm grateful you have some place safe to stay until the authorities catch him."

"You can stay here." Beth had almost forgotten Ms. Patti was in the room, until she spoke.

"Ms. Patti, while that would be great, you don't have the room. Not with Nica and Heath being here, along with me and Jamie. Brody told me Ridge and Shiloh are both going to be here soon. I appreciate the offer, but..."

Ms. Patti smiled, and Beth caught the calculating gleam in her eyes. She couldn't help wondering if Ms. Patti was up to something more than simply an offer of a bed for her friend.

"I actually meant Ms. Stewart could stay at Dane's house." She turned to Camilla. "Dane is our son. He runs the day-to-day operations of the ranch, and lives in the foreman's house here on the property. I'm sure he wouldn't mind sharing the space with you for a few days. There's plenty of room, as long as you don't mind being in a house with a few of my sons. Pretty sure Ridge will bunk there too, since the Big House is full up. Not sure about Shiloh's plans yet."

Beth hid a smirk behind her hand at the Machiavellian manipulation Ms. Patti employed, neatly boxing Camilla into a corner. Camilla's wild-eyed stare resembled a deer caught in the headlights of an oncoming semi, but there wouldn't be any wriggling off Ms. Patti's neatly baited hook. Good, she thought. Camilla needed a good shake-up to her life, and being around so many Boudreau men might be exactly what her friend needed.

"I...um...are you sure they won't mind my staying? I mean, I'm a stranger. Maybe this isn't the best idea. I can get a room—"

"Nonsense. It's settled. You visit with Beth. I'll go tell Dane he's got a new roommate. He or one of my other boys will be by in a bit to take your bag to the foreman's house." Ms. Patti grinned before adding, "Welcome to Shiloh Springs."

Beth couldn't hold back her laugh after Ms. Patti got out of earshot. She laughed until her sides hurt, and she was bent over, trying to catch her breath. Camilla looked shell-shocked. Beth knew the feeling, because she'd been treated to Ms. Patti's take-no-prisoners approach more than once when she'd first visited Tessa.

"What just happened?" Camilla stared through the opening between the kitchen and living area, a bemused expression on her face.

"You met the real Patricia Boudreau. She likes you. Trust me, if she didn't, you'd be back in your rental, headed toward Austin." She hooked her arm through Camilla's. "Now, no more games. Tell me why you're really here."

CHAPTER SIXTEEN

The day had dragged on forever, with one thing after the next pulling Brody away from the only place he wanted to be. With Beth. Questioning Greg revealed little more than he'd already known and did nothing toward pointing him toward who might be behind torching the Summers' barn. The only enlightening moment had been Greg revealing he'd kept up the insurance payments on the family home and property without his parents knowing. That put an interesting twist on the possibility the arson was motivated by money. And he was well aware people did a lot of crazy things out of greed.

He'd met Jeff back at the Summers' barn, and surveyed the added damage, and helped collect new evidence. Jeff had volunteered to drive it to the lab in Austin on Monday. Might be a good idea, because Brody didn't want to leave Beth, not while Evan remained free. He'd played a part in catching Evan and his buddy, Trevor, when they'd kidnapped Tessa. Whether it was luck or providence or fate, Brody had been the one to witness the two men strong-arm Tessa into their car. He'd been the one to contact Rafe, and followed them to the elementary school where Evan had taken Tessa. He seriously doubted Evan forgot about Brody's role in his arrest. And Evan didn't strike him as a forgive-and-forget kind of guy.

With a sigh, he pulled up in front of the Big House, spotting the white sedan with a rental sticker in the back window. *Wonder who's here?*

He'd barely made up halfway up the walk before Beth opened the front door. The rapid beating of his heart when he saw her sped up even faster at the sight of her smile. He barely refrained from sprinting to meet her at the front door. Instead, he maintained his steady gait, capturing her hands in his, and squeezing them.

"You look beautiful."

"Thanks."

He loved the flush of pink in her cheeks at the compliment. "Everything go okay today?"

"Other than Evan still being out there somewhere, it's been pretty quiet. Oh, my friend, Camilla, is here. Just so you know, she's Evan's sister."

He couldn't quite hide his frown. "What's she doing here? Did she know about his escape?"

"She's here because I invited her to visit. She'd planned to come to Texas anyway, because there were some papers she needed her brother to sign, and he's been stonewalling her. I don't know what they are, and I really don't care. But she was going to stay with me. When she offered to stay at a hotel, your mother graciously offered to let her stay here—at the foreman's house."

Brody didn't even try to hold back his laugh. "Bet Dane appreciated that bit of news."

"I haven't seen him yet, but Douglas got here a few minutes ago, and he took Camilla over there to drop off her bag and freshen up. They'll be back in time for dinner. Or as your brother Heath called it, supper. He showed up this morning, and finagled your mother into making chicken fried steak."

"Now that I believe. Heath has an unhealthy obsession with chicken fried steak for some reason. I swear he'd eat it for every meal if Momma would make it."

Hoping for a few minutes together before joining the rowdy bunch he could hear inside, he asked, "Feel like taking a walk before dinner?"

"I'd love to." She kept one hand in his as they stepped off the porch. He liked she felt comfortable enough to hold his hand. Maybe their botched first date attempt hadn't ruined any chance for them, if he was lucky.

Making a split-second decision, he headed for one place on the ranch he knew she'd never been. It was a special place, one most people outside the family didn't know existed, and he felt an uncontrollable urge to share it with Beth. See if she felt the undefinable pull toward it—toward him—he felt for her.

He led her around the side of the house, skirting a patio

and continued walking until they came upon a small deck in front of a set of French doors. Decorative urns and pots overflowed with green ferns and vividly colored flowers in pots scattered over the concrete surface. Comfortable-looking chairs and a glass table to the side completed the charming vignette.

He heard her indrawn breath as soon as she spotted where they were headed. A white-roofed gazebo sat in the clearing, surrounded by tall pine trees. While it wasn't huge, it was more than large enough to hold a dozen people comfortably. White lattice skirted the bottom, and a circular roof perched over the top. It reminded him of a woodland paradise, a hideaway in the middle of Texas, hidden away from prying eyes. He knew it was incongruent with a working Texas ranch, but his father had made this place, a special gift for his wife many years before.

Intertwined around the base of the gazebo, climbing pink and white roses and tall ornamental grasses grew in abundance, adding to its ethereal appearance, the air perfumed with the heady scent of the flowers, mixed with the earthy scent of the wooded area surrounding it.

Inside the gazebo, hidden in its depths was the big reveal, something surprising and unexpected. A well. When he'd been growing up, he and his brothers had called it the wishing well. He'd dropped more than a small amount of his allowance into its depths, hoping against hope for his desires to come true. Smooth stone encased the well itself, polished smooth with the age and the elements. The rocks weren't shiny and brand new. They were aged and weathered to a natural beauty. It should have seemed out of place inside the wooden structure, but somehow it fit.

Tiny white lights ringed around the tree trunks and along the inside of the circular roof line of the gazebo. Brody reached inside the entrance and flipped a switch, the lights turned on, illuminating the area in a warm glow, making it feel like something out of a dreamscape.

"Brody, this is amazing." Beth's hand smoothed along the painted wood, her fingertips barely touching it, as if afraid to break the spell of the secret garden.

"This," he gestured around, the sweep of his arm encompassing the whole area, "is Momma's secret garden. Dad built it for her as a surprise a couple of years after they moved here. He cleared the land and built the structure, but she did the rest. Planted all the flowers and the ornamental grasses, stringing the lights, everything."

Beth's face turned up to his, her eyes shiny with unshed tears. "This is an expression of love. You can feel it in every inch. Every flower."

He reached up and caught a tear with his thumb. "I didn't bring you here to make you cry."

Shaking her head, she laughed softly. "They aren't sad tears. It's just, seeing something like this, knowing the sentiment behind it, I can feel the love. Can't you?"

"Yes." The word broke forth and he knew he meant it,

but not in the way she thought. He knew Douglas and Ms. Patti loved each other. Sometimes it was like watching two teenagers, they were so giddy with it. No, he meant it for her. Beth. The woman who'd inched her way into his heart a little bit at a time, until he couldn't imagine his life without her. Without Jamie. They were a package deal and he wanted them both.

Beth climbed the step into the gazebo and stood looking down into the wishing well. Dusk had fallen, seeming to wrap them in a cloak of invisibility, where there wasn't anyone around except him and Beth. He knew there were people in the Big House, within shouting distance, yet right here, right now, they were the only two people in the whole world.

"Thank you for bringing me out here, and showing me this beautiful place. I hope Ms. Patti won't mind."

"She'll be fine with you seeing her garden and the gazebo. It's a place she only shares with people she cares about, and you are definitely one."

Reaching into his pocket, he pulled out a quarter and handed it to Beth. "Make a wish."

Her lips curved up in a smile. "Really? Think it'll work?"

"You'll never know unless you give it a try."

She closed her eyes for a few seconds, then tossed the coin. Stepping close to her, he wrapped his arms around her, pulling her against him, and held her. Simply let the night breeze embrace them, and enjoyed the stillness of the moment. Everything had been crazy for the last few days, and he knew they both needed a moment or two of being able to simply stop and take a deep breath. He was surprised when she leaned back against him, snuggling into his arms.

"This is nice," she whispered.

"Yes, it is."

She turned in his arms, and wrapped hers around his neck. "I'm sorry our date got ruined."

"It wasn't your fault. But we're here now, together." Reaching up with one hand, he brushed a lock of hair behind her ear, allowing his fingertips to glide across the silky skin of her cheek.

"Brody, I want…" Her words trailed off and her eyelids lowered, shielding her gaze. "Never mind."

He lifted her chin with his knuckle, and her eyes opened, meeting his. "Tell me, Beth."

"I want you to kiss me."

"My pleasure, sweetheart." Leaning down, he brushed his lips across hers, gentle at first, but deepened the kiss when he felt her response. He seemed to come alive inside, as if he'd been sleepwalking through life and only now was finally awake. It grew more intimate as his tongue traced along the seam of her lips, and she opened to him, making him feel ten feet tall.

The kiss ended with a gasp as they pulled apart, and he rested his forehead against hers.

"Wow." Her voice was breathless.

"Wow, indeed."

"Seems a shame we waited so long. Maybe we should do it again sometime?" The twinkle in her eyes matched the tone in her voice, light and teasing. A matching grin curved her full, just-kissed lips.

"Why wait?" He took her mouth in a devouring kiss, his hands cupping her face. Everything inside him seemed to click into place. This was what he wanted, what he'd been searching for without even realizing a piece of him had been missing.

Lifting his lips from hers, he trailed a line of kisses along her throat. Beth tipped her head to the side, her eyes sliding closed, and she tangled a hand in his hair. He worked his way back to her lips, devouring them, and deepening the kiss until they were both breathless. He drew his mouth along the skin under her ear, and down her neck, over her collarbone. Her skin was soft, silken, and perfect beneath his lips.

"Brody…" The words were a plea for more and he'd gladly give it. Give in to the desire rocketing through him. Make love to her until—

"Brody, you and Beth come in. Time for supper." Ms. Patti's voice broke them apart, and Beth stepped back, giggling like a schoolgirl who'd been caught doing something naughty. Her hands slapped across her mouth, trying to hold back her laughter.

"Momma's timing could use a little work. Though she's

right, we shouldn't be outside too long. Not with your ex still out there. It's not safe."

Beth leaned her head against his shoulder. "I always feel safe with you, Brody. We probably should go in, though. Thank you for sharing this beautiful place with me."

"My pleasure. All of it." In the glow of the twinkle lights, he watched pink suffuse her cheeks, knew she got the double entendre. "We'll have to do it again sometime."

"I think I'd like that."

CHAPTER SEVENTEEN

Evan pulled the stolen car onto a dirt-and-rock encrusted path, a barely visible road out in the middle of nowhere. He'd been avoiding anywhere people might be around, knowing his face was probably plastered all over the news. Anybody owning a television must've seen his mugshot by now. Between TV, the internet, and social media these days, he'd be lucky to stay off the grid for any length of time. He hoped it would be long enough to finish what he needed to do.

He'd wandered through a couple of suburban backyards, definitely well outside the outskirts of town, where houses weren't close together, spotting a few snot-nosed kids playing behind fences. But then again, he hadn't seen a lot of fences in this Podunk small town. Guess people didn't crave the privacy like the bigger cities. Not his cup of tea; he'd much rather live it up with loud music, wild nightlife, big cities, with bars, and lots of liquor. Maybe a couple of hookers. Prison had severely restricted his access to female companionship.

People must be more trusting in Middle America, too,

because he'd discovered a whole lot of unlocked back doors while he'd been snooping around, scouting Beth's location. He'd managed to enter a couple of houses without being spotted, grabbed clean clothes and food. Who'd have figured he'd turn into a halfway decent thief?

Too bad Beth hadn't been where she was supposed to be. He'd kept watch over the address of the apartment he'd been given, but he hadn't spotted her or his daughter. But his luck turned when a woman in a rusty older compact sedan pulled in and started unloading groceries. The idiot obviously didn't know a thing about the cardinal rule—never leave your keys in the ignition. Of course, he benefitted from her mistake, because he didn't have a clue how to hotwire a car. Not a skill set he'd ever thought he'd need. When she'd foolishly walked toward the building's entrance, he sprinted across the parking lot, slid behind the wheel, and sped away, easy-peasy.

Where is Beth?

He drove as far as he could down the barely negotiable path, needing to get off the road for a while. By now, the woman had probably reported her car stolen, and the last thing he needed was to be pulled over by the cops.

Especially that lousy sheriff, Rafe Boudreau.

Oh yeah, he had a score to settle with the good sheriff. He was top three on his list, along with his brother. He couldn't comprehend what Tessa saw in the sheriff, with his cornpone, aw shucks personality.

Grabbing a couple of branches off the ground, he stacked them around the rear bumper of the car, obscuring it from view as best he could with the leaves mostly brown and brittle. They blended right in with the pockets of rust on this hunk of junk. He pocketed the keys and climbed into the back seat, stretching out on the cushioned bench seat. He needed to lay low for an hour or two, catch a catnap and then try to sneak back to the apartment complex.

Time was running out. He could practically hear a clock ticking in his head. As much as he wanted to think the cops were inept, between the local cops and the feds, and who knows whoever else looking for him, he needed to grab Beth, get money, and head as far away from this disaster as possible.

Closing his eyes, his lips curled up in a smile at the thought of Beth at his mercy. Revenge would be oh…so…sweet.

Brody answered the phone on the first ring. He'd been on edge most of the night, antsy to get back to the Big House. Back to Beth. Checking in with Rafe the night before, he'd slammed his fist against the wall when his brother told him there still wasn't any info on Evan. The man was a city dude. How was he able to survive in rural Texas without somebody spotting him?

"Tell me you've heard something?"

"Good morning to you too, grouch." Rafe's cheerful voice made him wince, especially since he hadn't had his first cup of coffee yet.

"I am not in the mood for your crap today, Rafe. Tell me what's going on with Stewart."

"From the feds, nothing. Same with the state troopers. But I did receive report of a stolen car."

"Where?" Brody stood straighter, getting a gut feeling.

"Here. In the county, but not in town. The reason I think it's significant is because it was stolen from the apartment complex where Beth and Jamie used to live until a few days ago."

"It's him."

"I think so. Enough to pass the information on to everyone else. Antonio called SAC Williamson, who told him to stick around Shiloh Springs until Stewart is apprehended. He's heading this way too. Personally, I think he wants to see Daisy again."

"Yeah, well, tell him to flirt on his own time. We need to find Stewart."

He was here, Brody could feel it. That sick, twisted freak was in Shiloh Springs, which meant he'd come for Beth. Not gonna happen. He'd die before he let Stewart get his hands on Beth or Jamie.

"Where are you?"

"Back at my place," Brody answered. "There were

enough people crowded into the Big House last night, so Momma told me to come back this morning. She's keeping everybody home from church, in case Stewart shows up."

"Lemme ask you something, bro. What do you make of Stewart's sister showing up? Too much of a coincidence?"

Brody immediately understood Rafe's concern, because he'd instinctively felt the same when he'd found out Camilla Stewart showed up in Shiloh Springs. Even with advance notice, and Beth saying it was okay, it seemed too good to be true Stewart's sister would be on a plane to Texas the day after he escaped from Huntsville Prison.

"Beth swears Camilla is nothing like her brother. She knew Camilla was coming to Texas, and she was going to spend a couple of days with her and Jamie. Apparently, she had some papers Stewart needed to sign, and he'd been balking, so she decided to show up in person and make him sign them."

"That's what Beth told me too, but something doesn't feel right. It's got my Spidey senses tingling."

Brody chuckled at his brother's half-hearted joke, though he trusted Rafe's instincts. His brother had instincts when it came to bad guys and seemed to have a sixth sense when it came to figuring out the criminal mindset, and how to deal with miscreants.

"If he's here, close enough to be at her apartment, then I need to get back to the Big House."

"I figured you'd say that. I'm pulling up to the apartment complex now. I want to talk to the lady whose car was stolen. It hasn't been sighted yet, but he can't stay hidden forever. Dusty's gonna drive by Old Man Johnson's cottage, check and make sure nobody's been snooping around looking for Beth and Jamie."

"Keep me posted."

"You got it. Talk to you later."

Brody hung up and headed for the kitchen. His apartment wasn't big, only a one bedroom, but it was enough until he settled down. He'd tried living in Austin, figuring he'd spread his wings outside Shiloh Springs. Not his brightest idea. Within a year, he was back. The furniture he'd splurged on when moving he'd placed in storage, until Tessa's place had been trashed. He'd loaned it willingly. What good did it do sitting in a storage unit gathering dust? Now it was at the Old Johnson place, where Beth and Jamie lived. He liked the thought of them sitting on his furniture, making a home with things he'd picked out. Maybe someday...

He dumped grounds into the coffee maker, added the water and turned it on. Despite what everybody said, he didn't really care for those pod-type coffee makers. There was something satisfying about being able to measure out the grounds and watching while it brewed. This morning, he needed the sharp kick of caffeine. He'd barely slept, thinking about Beth and their kiss.

It had been exactly how he'd imagined it. He wasn't sure

when their friendship had started growing into something more. Something special. Now he wished he hadn't wasted so much time worrying about what others would think, whether they'd approve. So much time lost he'd never get back. But he refused to dwell in the past any longer.

He loved Beth. It had snuck up on him, but didn't change the fact. He was head-over-heels, totally and deeply in love with the woman, and he didn't care who knew. Things would change once Stewart was back behind bars. The good thing was this stunt he'd pulled would add a whole new batch of charges against him, and he'd be spending the rest of his foreseeable future being bunk mates with the rest of the male population of Huntsville. He was pretty sure this time, Stewart wouldn't be getting out so easily.

The text alert pinged on his phone, and he swiped the message open. The lab tech had texted he'd sent an e-mail with the findings Brody was waiting for. There it was, in black and white. The forensic lab confirmed the fire at the Summers' barn was deliberate.

Arson.

He read through the rest of the report, frowning. As he'd suspected, gasoline had been the accelerant used. Not much help, because gasoline was readily available, a cheap and easy source. They'd tested the charred wood samples, as well as the broken pieces of glass, the ones that hadn't been sent to the crime lab to look for any DNA or fingerprints. Hopefully he'd get their report within the next day or two. Since it was

Sunday, he was lucky he'd gotten the lab report. It was too much to hope for a twofer.

He'd let Greg know as well as the insurance company. Greg had headed back to San Antonio after answering his questions, depressed and worried his family's property was being targeted by an unknown person. This was going to devastate that family, and he felt guilty he had to share the bad news with them. But it was his job, his responsibility. On the bright side, if you could call it a bright side, this confirmed there was a serial arsonist working in Shiloh Springs.

The real job was just beginning.

CHAPTER EIGHTEEN

Even with everything going on around her, Beth felt like she was walking on air. Brody had kissed her! And what a kiss! It had curled her toes and made her feel all tingly inside. She took the stairs two at a time, practically skipping her way to the kitchen. Pulling up short, she spotted Heath seated at the table, a mug of coffee in one hand and a tablet in the other. A frown of concentration marred his otherwise handsome features.

"Good morning." His voice rumbled before he took a deep swallow of coffee. "Momma left breakfast warming in the oven. Said she had a couple of things she had to do this morning, but she'll be back."

"Thanks." Pouring her own cup, she took a sip, and looked out the window over the sink. Bright sunlight shone on the back vegetable garden, and she could see one of the barn cats sneaking across the grass. She smiled, knowing the first thing Jamie would want to do was head out to play with the kittens. With all the excitement of the last couple of days, she'd left her sleeping upstairs.

Laying his tablet on the table, Heath studied her, before

propping his elbows on the table and resting his chin on his hands. "I had a long talk with Dad last night. He explained to me what's been going on. Anything I can do to help?"

Beth slid onto the chair across from Heath. "Everybody's doing what they can. Rafe's got the locals keeping watch for Evan. Antonio's dealing with the FBI. He told me Mr. Williamson, his boss, wants him to stick around Shiloh Springs until Evan's captured. I really hope he's caught soon, so everybody can go back to their normal lives." Her hands tightened around the mug, and she whispered, "I hate this. My problems have turned everybody else's lives upside down."

"Tell me what your gut feels, Beth. Do you think Evan will run for the border, maybe head to another state?"

She shook her head. "He'll come after me. He hates me for not standing by him when he was arrested. I'm not sure what he expected—he tried to kill my sister! Planned to kill me. All for money. Somehow in his twisted logic, he thinks I'm the bad guy because I gave it all away. Except he doesn't believe I gave it to the county. He thinks I keep a big chunk for myself." She gave a bitter laugh. "He's the one who got us into so much financial trouble I may never be able to dig myself out of the hole he created."

"From what I've read of his depositions and his plea deal, that's the impression I got too. He's narcissistic. He has delusions of grandeur. Thinks he's above everyone else, including being above the law. Sound right?"

"You've pretty much pegged him. I can't believe how blind I was. Maybe I deluded myself, because he was so different when we first met. Even when we first married. I thought I had the perfect marriage. Which goes to show how big a fool I am."

"I don't know you. Haven't got a clue who or what you're all about. But I know my family wouldn't take you in, wouldn't consider you part of it, if you were a fool. Brody wouldn't care for you if he considered you unworthy. And my parents are good judges of character."

"They only know me because of Tessa."

Heath slowly shook his head. "They met you through your sister, true. But they care about you because you're a good person—or so I'm told. You're a loving mother who'd do anything to protect her child. You're raising her on your own. You picked up and moved halfway across the country to start over. I wouldn't call that a fool. I'd call that a strong, determined woman who can do anything she sets her mind to."

Beth met his stare straight on. "You are definitely a Boudreau."

A beautiful smile changed Heath's entire face, taking him from slightly dangerous to stunning. "A name I proudly claim." Standing, he walked to the coffee pot and poured another cup. "I'm not the type to pussyfoot around, so I'm going to ask you outright. What are your feelings for my brother?"

"Brody?"

"Yeah, Brody. Momma said you're his." He made the statement sound like it was a done deal.

"I…we're…feeling our way. He's been a very good friend."

"Is that all he is to you—a friend? Because if all you feel is friendship, tell him. Don't play coy or toy with him, he deserves better."

Beth jerked back at the vehemence in Heath's voice. It was obvious he cared about his brother, and didn't want to see him hurt. Wasn't it a good thing she had no intention of hurting him?

"I would never intentionally hurt Brody. I care about him a great deal."

"Bah, I hate wishy-washy sentimentality. Either you love him or you don't."

Beth's eyes widened at the anger on Heath's face, but somehow, she knew it wasn't directed at her. Somebody'd hurt him badly in the past, and he still carried the scars.

"What is between Brody and me is personal and it's private. All I can say is I'll never intentionally break his heart."

Heath studied her face, weighing her words. Finally, he took a deep breath and nodded. "Good enough."

Beth let out the breath she hadn't realized she'd been holding. "You sure I can't get you some breakfast? Suddenly, I'm starving."

Heath chuckled and nodded, grinning. "Sounds good."

Brody had barely climbed behind the wheel of his pickup when his phone rang. Blasted thing wouldn't stop pinging this morning. Messages from the Austin lab. Rafe. The fire station. Everybody kept pestering him when all he wanted was to drive out to the Big House and see Beth. Especially knowing Stewart might have been in Shiloh Springs, he wanted—needed—to keep her and Jamie safe.

"What?"

"Boss, got another fire. A bad one." Jeff Barnes' voice was low and serious, enough so Brody felt a surge of adrenaline spike through his blood. Brody scrubbed a hand across his face, barely refraining from banging his head against the steering wheel. This day kept getting better and better.

"Where?"

"Santiago's, the old Tex-Mex restaurant, the one that closed a few months ago. Crews on site, but it's a bad one." Jeff's voice lowered perceptibly before adding, "I think it might be arson."

Brody let loose a string of curses, frustration eating away at what little control he had remaining. Things were escalating if the arsonist had struck again. It had been less than twenty-four hours since they'd struck the Summers' barn for the second time, now this?

"I'm on my way. Call in extra backup if you need it from Burnet County."

"I'm on it, Boss."

Brody pulled out of the apartment drive and headed west. Santiago's was located about twenty minutes or so from where he lived, and he stomped on the gas, hoping to cut that time in half. The restaurant had closed a few months ago. Brody knew they'd had trouble with a variety of things, including failing health inspections. It also wasn't in the best location for foot traffic and tourists, not being in the city. Matter of fact, he was surprised it had stayed open this long, although it had been popular with the high school crowd on Friday and Saturday nights. Trucks full of teens would drive there, load up with to-go bags and then head out for the lake. More than once they'd been called in to douse bonfires left unattended by that crowd. Businesses couldn't sustain itself with that kind of clientele, which probably led to their closure.

Black plumes of smoke spiraled upward the closer he got. Jeff hadn't exaggerated the seriousness of the blaze, and he anticipated needing the additional support from the next county. He maintained a good relationship with the fire chief in Burnet County, and they had a mutually agreed plan of assistance any time it was needed. Looked like this morning they'd be taking advantage of that.

Slamming on his brakes, he raced from his car toward

the area where he spotted Jeff, giving orders and directing the men of his company. The Burnet Company worked side-by-side with his team, rallying to contain the fire and keep it from spreading. Fortunately, there weren't any nearby buildings to catch fire, but the tree line behind the restaurant was rife with downed branches and bushes desperately in need of water. It was a sad fact Texas was in the midst of a dry spell, and a lot of people were praying for rain. The natural vegetation alongside roadways and in unincorporated areas was especially hard hit, dry and brittle. A perfect conduit for sparks to ignite into out-of-control blazes.

"Hey, Boss. Burnet County FD is handling the western half of the building, and we're containing the right side. Two-in, two-out teams are checking for anyone inside. So far, no casualties. Burnet has another tanker on the way."

"Good. Who called it in?"

"Anonymous nine-one-one call. Only on the line long enough to report the fire, then hung up."

"Got it." Brody surveyed his surroundings, watching his men work in a synchronized, well-organized fashion that might appear chaotic to civilians, but each member of his company knew their job, their responsibility, and performed their assigned tasks with exacting precision. Huge plumes of water sprayed the building, attacking from both directions. The flames, which had been shooting skyward when he'd arrived, were already diminishing, being contained by the men and women ringing the building.

He spotted Burnet's captain and jogged over to meet him, waiting while he radioed information to his company. The firefighters from the neighboring county worked well, right alongside his own men and women, and he felt a surge of pride even with a company as small as Shiloh Springs, they performed on a level most smaller stations couldn't match. All the extra hours of training, learning to work as a unit, paid off as the fire inside the restaurant was contained.

"Thanks for helping out. Things could have gone south pretty quick."

Burnet's captain nodded, shaking Brody's outstretched hand. "Glad we could help. Rotten way to start a Sunday, though."

"Yeah, it is. What's your impression? You've been on scene longer than me. What started this?"

Brody watched the other man closely, noted the slight tightening of his muscles, the stiffening of his spine. He could almost quote verbatim what the other man would say, but he figured he'd at least see if his suspicions were correct.

"Hard to tell without getting a chance to examine the scene, once the fire's out."

Noncommittal. Exactly how he'd have answered, if questioned by somebody you didn't know well. "I've got a reason for asking. I'd like your gut instinct, just between you and me."

"As fast as the structure burned, my first thought would be deliberately set." He held up a hand before he continued,

"Now there are a lot of variables to take into account. Gas lines. Faulty equipment still inside the restaurant. Illegal electrical wiring. You know as well as I do, the list is endless. Without a thorough examination of the scene, I wouldn't presume to toss out a definite cause."

"Understood. Appreciate your expertise and your opinion."

"You having a problem in Shiloh Springs? Anything I need to be concerned with, that might spill over into my county?"

Brody hesitated for a heartbeat before answering. "We've had a couple of suspicious burns in the last few months. Just got back the findings from the state lab on the latest. Confirmed as intentional. I doubt it's anything y'all need to worry about, but it wouldn't hurt to keep your eyes and ears open. I'll update you if I find out anything concrete."

"Think you might have a firebug, huh? That sucks. Appreciate it if you'd keep us in the loop. Lemme know if there's anything we can help with."

"I keep you updated. And thanks for the assist," Brody added, gesturing toward the smoldering building. "Got this under control fast. Always a good thing."

As he started to walk away, back to his crew, his phone dinged. He snagged it out of his pocket, sorely tempted to toss it into the still smoldering building, but stopped cold when he spotted the e-mail sender's name. Swiping right, he read the message, feeling the knot in the pit of his stomach growing. The Forensic Arson Crime Lab had found two fingerprints on the glass fragments collected at the Summers' scene, one full and one partial.

He closed his eyes and took a deep breath before opening the attached file. Skimming through the usual rigamarole, stuff the arson lab had already reported to him about the accelerant use, until he zeroed in on the one thing that mattered, the analysis of the fingerprint evidence. The Texas DPS had run the prints and had a match.

He had a suspect, a flesh-and-blood villain to focus the blame on. Somebody who could be arrested and thrown in jail. But first, he had to finish dealing with the current blaze, and ensure the fire was out and not a danger to life or property. Focus on doing his job.

Then he'd arrest the person who'd been behind torching the Summers' property.

Greg Summers.

Evan bit down hard on the hamburger he'd grabbed from a drive-through fast-food place, one of those big chain ones where nobody paid attention to who moved past their congested drive-up window, as long as they paid and got moving, so they could attend to the next customer. Compared to the lousy food he'd eaten in the prison, this tasted like a gourmet steak.

He'd driven out of town, over an hour away from Shiloh Springs, clear into the next county, staying on the backroads to avoid any patrol cars who might have spotted him. Pouring some of his previous bottled water onto the ground, he'd made enough mud to coat the back and front license plates, partially obscuring the letters and numbers. A cop probably wouldn't pull somebody over for that, not unless they spotted another infraction, and he'd been careful to stay under the speed limit and do nothing to draw attention to himself.

Now, with a full tank of gas and a full belly, he cruised by the cottage where one of Beth's former neighbors at the apartment complex told him they'd moved to. It wasn't much of a place. He'd have thought his ex would have splurged a little with all the money she'd gained from all his hard work. Even splitting the proceeds with her sister, she still should have had a couple of million bucks stashed away. Surely she could afford something better than this dump.

He had the forethought to park a few houses down, because he didn't want Beth to spot him too soon. The timing had to be perfect, because he'd only get one shot. Too bad it was Sunday, because even if she wired money to his account—one nobody but him knew about—it wouldn't process until Monday at the earliest, maybe Tuesday, so he had to be patient.

In the rearview mirror, he spotted a white sedan driving slowly toward him, and he scrunched down in the seat, obscuring him from immediate view. There was no disguising that white car as anything but a cop car, even in this backwater burb. They continued on past, and he waited, knowing if he got up too soon and blew it, he'd end up back in Huntsville, this time in solitary.

Once he had the money, he'd leave. He had it all plotted out. There was a lovely seaside bungalow in Rio calling to him. With Beth's share of the bond, he could live comfortably for many years, without encumbrances like a wife and a child. He felt a twinge of guilt thinking about Jamie. It was a shame she'd be dragged into this because her mother betrayed him.

The white sedan pulled into the drive of Beth's cottage, and a tall man in a tan shirt and dark pants stepped out, walking slowly around the side of the house, disappearing from view. Definitely a cop, from the way he walked and the way he carried himself. A thief wouldn't have pulled right up into the drive and gotten out; he'd learned that much while incarcerated. Keeping his head low, he watched and waited. Long minutes passed before the cop came around the other side of the house, his long strides now purposeful as he walked to his car, climbed in and pulled away.

Shifting to sit upright behind the wheel, he took another bite of his now cold burger, before wrapping it up and tossing it into the trash bag. He took a long drink of the milkshake he'd gotten to go with the burger and added it to the trash.

Movement from the side caught his attention, and he watched an older woman carrying a black trash bag out of her house and head toward one of the bins standing at attention like soldiers at the side of her drive. Taking a quick glance in the mirror again, he made an attempt to smooth his hair, and scrubbed a hand across his scruff, and opened the car door.

"Excuse me, ma'am. I'm hoping you can help me."

"What can I do for you?" She hesitated, watching him closely as he moved a few steps into her driveway.

"I'm looking for a friend who recently moved into this area. I know she's renting a place on this street, but I can't for the life of me find the paper I wrote her address down on. Maybe you know her? Beth Stewart?"

The woman's face lit with a smile. "Oh, of course. Such a lovely lady, and sweet little girl, too. She hasn't been here long, but she lives right over there." She pointed to the cottage Evan had been staking out. "Although I heard there was a spot of trouble, and she's been staying with the Boudreaus."

"Boudreaus?"

"They own the big ranch outside town. Biggest one around for miles. Just follow Main Street through town, and keep heading north. You can't miss it."

Evan seethed, gritting his teeth in a semblance of a smile. Looked like his wife had gotten further ensnared by the Boudreaus, the same way Tessa got pulled in. Good thing he planned on putting a stop to that, once and for all.

"Thank you, ma'am. Appreciate your help. I'll try and catch up with her later."

Giving the woman a final wave, Evan marched back to his stolen car and climbed behind the wheel. It wouldn't be long before he had everything he wanted, and having a chance to get even with the Boudreaus was the cherry on top.

With a wicked grin, he started the ignition and drove off, heading for Main Street.

CHAPTER NINETEEN

Beth knew everyone wanted her to stay inside the house, but she was getting cabin fever, going stir-crazy, being cooped up inside. She hadn't heard from Brody, and she missed him. Missed the cheeky half-grin he had, the right side of his lips curving slightly higher than the left. Missed feeling his arms wrapped around her. And she secretly missed his need to protect her. Not that she was a shrinking violet or anything, but his overprotectiveness made her feel cherished. Special. Something she hadn't felt in a long time.

Jamie was upstairs taking a nap—finally. She'd been running around the ranch since she'd woken up. Beth had given in and let her have waffles for breakfast, and then they'd headed out to the barn to visit the kittens. Afterward, Jamie had insisted Beth meet Otto, the donkey. Her brave little girl had climbed up the wooden fence running beside the barn and called Otto to her side, laughing as she scratched him between the ears. Unfortunately, Otto hadn't taken to Beth's attempts to pet him, barring his yellowed teeth and braying in an ear-splitting sound that had her slamming her hands over her ears.

They'd then spent time in Ms. Patti's vegetable garden behind the kitchen, watering the plants, and pulling the occasional weed, though Beth admitted there weren't very many. This was a well-tended garden.

She'd worked a little with Jamie on her lessons. Even pre-kindergarten classes had lessons and Mrs. Gleason had e-mailed her information of things she could work on with Jamie, so she didn't fall even further behind. Between the move from North Carolina and now this enforced isolation at the Big House, Beth was afraid Jamie was going to have to repeat the school year.

Nica had volunteered to keep an eye on Jamie to give Beth a break, and she'd decided to visit with Camilla, who'd set up a mini-office at Dane's house. Working remotely wasn't a problem for Camilla, who could do her job anywhere she had access to a computer and Wi-Fi. She'd figured as long as Evan was on the run, she'd stay close to Beth and Jamie.

Since it was a beautiful day, if a little warm, Beth decided to walk to Dane's house. Nica had given her directions, which seemed pretty straightforward. The walk shouldn't take long, but getting out and getting some fresh air would be nice. Skirting around the back of the barn, she followed Nica's directions, enjoying the bucolic scenery and peaceful contentment the ranch provided. She paused to watch the horses munching on the alfalfa, the mommas and babies frolicking in the grass. Having never been around farm animals before, observing them offered her a rare insight into Brody's life growing up. Made her feel like she was getting a snapshot of where he'd come from.

Tessa had explained to her about the Boudreaus when she first started seeing Rafe seriously. How each of the boys raised by the Boudreau family had come to them from horrible life situations or through the foster care system. She didn't know any specific details, not even Rafe's, though she knew Tessa did. It wasn't her business, but she couldn't help wondering about Brody's story. What had his life been like before he'd moved in with Douglas and Ms. Patti?

There was no doubt he adored his adoptive parents and they loved him. That wasn't even an issue. She knew while most of the boys had been officially adopted, some of them hadn't, whether because they couldn't be, or because it was a mutual decision, there wasn't a single doubt the love shared between not only Douglas and Ms. Patti, but with all of the brothers, was something unique and strong. They were the epitome of family.

The Big House soon disappeared from view as she continued her walk to the foreman's house. Birdsong filled the air, and Beth smiled at the peace she felt inside. Most likely it was the calm before the storm, because Evan didn't allow her even a brief respite, but she'd take the small moments when and where she could. Once he was back in prison, she was cutting all ties with him, once and for all. No more phone calls, no letters. Nothing.

In the distance, she could see a white two-story house, with blue shutters and a gingerbread trim. A wide front porch, complete with a swing and columns, decorated the structure. It reminded her of photos she'd seen from the turn of the twentieth century, lovely and reminiscent of a bygone era. She chuckled, thinking about Camilla living in a farmhouse. There was nobody more citified than Camilla Stewart. Now there was a woman who loved her creature comforts. Spa days, mani-pedis, good wine, and fancy restaurants were more her speed than homespun life with the white picket fence and a couple of kids. This had to be pure torture for her friend.

Within a few minutes, she was standing on the porch, hand raised, when the front door was yanked inward, and a hand reached out, yanking her inside. She gasped at the sight in front of her. Camilla's hair stood on end, spiking out away from her face. Her feet were bare, pink toes sticking out from the bottom of her dust-covered slacks. Glasses were perched on the end of her nose, a wild look on her face.

"You've gotta get me out of here!"

"Camilla, what in the world? What's wrong?"

"What's wrong? What's right! I'm sorry, Beth, I love you and Jamie to death, but I can't stay here a second longer. This—this is torture!"

"Okay, calm down. What happened?"

"That gigantic, motorcycle-driving maniac happened. He makes me so mad! Ugh!"

Beth bit her lip to keep from laughing. Apparently, Camilla had met Heath. "I take it Heath's giving you trouble?"

"Heath? Is that what he's called? I figured his name was Neanderthal, since he's such a caveman. What a jerk!"

"Come on, Camilla. I've met him. He's a perfectly nice—"

"Are you kidding me? First, he used up all the hot water, so I couldn't take a shower." She started ticking items off on her fingers. "Then he drank the whole pot of coffee before I got up, leaving me caffeine deprived. You know I can't function without at least two cups first thing in the morning. Then he confiscated my laptop, and won't give it back!" Her voice rose with each infraction, until it reached a shrill screech. Beth barely kept from sticking her fingers in her ears.

"Whoa, calm down. I'm sure there's more hot water. You'll be able to take a shower. As for the coffee, come on, let's go to the kitchen and I'll make you a fresh pot."

Camilla sniffled. "You can't. Apparently, there's no more until Dane can make a grocery run or his mother drops by with supplies. I mean, seriously, who allows themselves to run out of coffee?! And it's not even the kind of coffeemaker with pods. You have to actually add the grounds. It's archaic."

"No, you're spoiled."

"Am not." Camilla slumped down in a chair and stuck her tongue out at Beth. "I'm sorry. This trip has been an utter fiasco. Every single step, from the moment I got the call about Evan, up until today with Captain Caveman, has been an unmitigated disaster. Except for seeing you and Jamie. You are the bright spot in my nightmare."

Beth sat across from Camilla, watching her friend's expression go from frantic to harried to finally calm. Camilla tended to be overly emotional, feeling things strongly and with no problem expressing her opinion. Apparently, she'd met her match in Heath Boudreau.

"Morning, sunshine." Heath ambled into the room, and tousled Beth's hair, giving a heated glance to Camilla, before heading to the refrigerator and pulling out a bottle of water. "How's Brody?"

Beth leaned back against her chair, and crossed her arms over her chest. "I haven't spoken with him today."

"He didn't spend the night?" Heat crept into her cheeks, burning hotter at Heath's chuckle. "Don't worry, I'm teasing." He pulled out another chair at the kitchen table and slid onto the seat. "I talked to him last night. He's got a lot on his plate right now, dealing with some stuff at the firehouse."

"I know. He's been working a lot of hours recently."

Camilla watched Heath, her expression guarded, but Beth could see the spark of interest Camilla did her best to hide. *Oh, brother, if these two get together, talk about fireworks.*

"Any word on your ex?"

She shook her head. "Nothing. I don't understand why

nobody's caught him yet. He doesn't know anything about surviving outside of the city."

Camilla gave an inelegant snort. "Got that right. Roughing it to Evan is staying any place with less than four stars. No way he'd be able to live off the land. He's too spoiled."

Heath arched one brow at Camilla. "Pot, meet kettle."

"I'll have you know I can take care of myself."

"Sure you can, princess. As long as you have a fancy pants boy toy to wait on you hand and foot, I'm sure you'd survive just fine."

"I'm going to take a shower. Beth, I'll see you in a few minutes." She glared at Heath. "You don't need to be here when I get back. And give me my computer, you big goober." With that final word, she stormed from the room, her footsteps fading as she climbed the stair.

"You really shouldn't give her such a hard time."

Heath grinned. "But she makes it so easy."

"Be that as it may, she's still reeling from her brother being sent to prison and having her life thrown into turmoil. She adored him, and it's hard to find out somebody you care about has feet of clay."

Heath's gaze shifted to the hallway where Camilla had disappeared, his expression guarded. "I'll try." He stood and tossed his plastic bottle into a bin under the sink. "You wouldn't happen to have a picture of your ex handy?"

She shook her head, starting to say no, but hesitated. "You have Camilla's computer?" At his quick nod, she added, "Let's look on her Facebook page. I'm sure there are lots of them on there."

"Lemme grab it, just a second." He returned quickly with the state-of-the-art laptop, and Beth quickly logged in, easily navigating to Camilla's page.

"This is Evan. Probably taken about a year ago, maybe a little more." She clicked on the photo, enlarging it. It showed a happy, smiling man, groomed and polished to perfection, the way she remembered him.

"Can you e-mail me a copy of that?" He rattled off his e-mail address, and Beth shot the photo to his phone, wondering why he wanted a copy. She hadn't realized she'd spoke her question aloud until he answered.

"I'm going to head into town, see if I can spot him. I know some people who might help. At least I'll feel like I'm doing something instead of simply sitting around, waiting for something to happen."

"Wish I could go too. I feel useless, being babysat by everybody else."

"You're not useless. You are protecting your child, and that's more important than you wandering around trying to find a needle in a haystack. You've got the important job. Let the rest of us find your ex and send him back to Huntsville."

"I know, I just hate feeling helpless. Before I met Evan, I was strong. I had confidence, knew who I was and what I wanted. Somehow, over the years, I've become…less. I feel like I've lost a part of me, of who I am."

Heath surprised her by leaning down and hugging her, a brief but tight squeeze. "The last thing I'd say about you is you're weak. It takes strength to stand up to a man and tell him no. You did that. From what my family has told me, when you and your sister found out what your ex-husband tried to do, you stood up to him. Divorced him. Protected your child. Gave the money back to the people of Crowley County. A weak-willed person wouldn't have done that. They'd have sat back and taken the money, lived a comfortable life, without a single lick of conscience. Nope," he ruffled her hair again, "you're a warrior woman. Brody's got his hands full."

Beth was speechless at Heath's words. Did he really see her like that? More importantly, did Brody see her as a strong, independent woman, and not the meek puppet Evan wanted?

"He's right." Camilla walked in, her gaze assessing Heath. She'd had a shower and now looked like the sophisticated, put together woman Beth was used to seeing, instead of the screaming harpy who'd answered the door.

"Of course I'm right."

Camilla ignored him, her stare focused on Beth. "I've always known you were incredible. But you proved just how much fortitude and willpower you possessed when you stood up for your convictions, doing the right thing. I never doubted your strength or your character, not for a second. Captain Caveman is right, you are a warrior. You just needed a chance to prove it."

"And with that, I'm out. I'll call the Big House if I hear anything."

Beth watched Heath walk away, and noticed her friend's eyes glued to the big man too, with a curiosity that piqued Beth's interest. Camilla had been hurt in the past, and stayed away from anything resembling a commitment. She dated, but played the field, never staying with any one man for more than a month or so before she moved on. If Camilla stuck around, who knew what might happen? Though she didn't know Heath, having just met him, she did know his family, and if he was anything like the rest of them, which she was pretty confident he was, Camilla could certainly do a lot worse.

"I see you got my laptop back from the Neanderthal. Hope he didn't screw up my files."

"Camilla, give the guy a break. He drove halfway across the country to see his family, only instead of getting to spend time with them, he's been plunged neck deep in my problems. I think he deserves the benefit of the doubt, okay?"

"Halfway across the country? West coast, I hope."

"Nope. Virginia. Actually works in D.C."

"No way he's a politician. He's not polished enough."

Beth shook her head. "I think he works for the ATF. All these Boudreau men seem to like high energy, uber-masculine jobs."

Camilla pushed her hair behind her shoulders and straightened. "Well, I still haven't had my caffeine. Want to head back to the Boudreau house and see if they've got some coffee?"

Before Beth could answer, her cell phone rang. Looking down at the caller ID, she noted Nica's name. "Nica, everything okay?

"Beth, I can't find Jamie. She's gone."

CHAPTER TWENTY

With the fire finally contained, Brody left Jeff in charge of clearing and processing the scene, and looking for evidence of foul play. Jeff had almost finished his courses, and this would be good on-the-job experience, though he'd follow up on everything he did, to make sure he didn't miss anything vital. In the meantime, though, he needed to head to the sheriff's station, and update Rafe on what the forensic arson crime lab uncovered about the Summers' fire.

How could Greg do this? The man flat-out lied to his face yesterday when he'd questioned him about his family's homestead. When he'd asked him if he could think of a single person who'd want to burn it, he'd said no. An awful thought raced through his mind, one he hadn't wanted to considered, even when he'd suspected Greg's involvement. Could Greg's family be in on it? Would they condone, maybe even orchestrate, the fire and subsequent coverup? It didn't seem plausible, but at this point, he wasn't sure about anything anymore.

Right now, he had more questions than answers. The only concrete thing he had was documented proof Greg's prints were found at the scene. He decided to take a deep breath and break down the facts. Number one, Greg had the means. Gasoline as an accelerant was quick, easy to obtain, and affordable. Anybody could drive up to a gas station and fill up a five-gallon container without arousing suspicion, especially in a small town like Shiloh Springs. Number two, Greg had motive. His family was in desperate need of a cash infusion. His mother's cancer treatments were mounting and expensive, draining the family's coffers dry. As a motive, it was hard to think of a better one. Paying for an ailing parent's chemotherapy and radiation therapy treatments might hold sway with jurors, compassionate circumstances notwithstanding. Number three, Greg had the opportunity to commit the crime. Though he lived in San Antonio, it wasn't that far a drive to Shiloh Springs. He could have done it and gotten back home before he'd been missed, with no one the wiser.

Pulling up in front of the sheriff's station, he sat with his hands wrapped around the steering wheel, gripping it until his knuckles turned white. He never minded putting a firebug behind bars. It was his job. His responsibility. Keeping people and their homes and property safe was something he took seriously. Yet now his conscious warred with his oath to protect. Greg was his friend. He'd known the family for more than twenty years.

With a heavy sigh, he climbed out of his truck and headed inside. He needed to talk to Rafe, get his head on straight before he did something he might regret. Sally Anne greeted him as he walked inside, though she seemed subdued, almost sad. He waved, but couldn't allow himself to be distracted. This needed to be handled now, before he headed for San Antonio and a confrontation with Greg.

After a perfunctory knock on Rafe's door, he opened it and stopped short, spotting Greg sitting across from Rafe. The seriousness in his brother's expression had the little hairs on the back of his neck standing at attention.

"What's going on?"

"Come in, Brody, and close the door." Rafe motioned to the chair beside Greg. "We have a situation."

"You have no idea," Brody muttered under his breath.

"Greg, you want to tell him or should I?"

Greg's shoulders slumped, and he couldn't quite meet Brody's gaze. "I'm turning myself in. I'm the one who set the fires."

Fires? Plural?

"Okay," he drawled out the word, his gaze shifting to Rafe.

"I've read Mr. Summers his rights, and he's waived his right to counsel. Greg, why don't you start at the beginning, and tell Brody what you told me." Rafe pointed to the recorder on his desk, and Brody raised his brows, looking at his brother.

"Like I told Rafe, I mean Sheriff Boudreau, I started the fire on our property. The barn. I was desperate. My dad was calling me all the time, moaning and groaning about how the land wouldn't sell, how he needed the money for Mom's treatments. I'm overextended. My savings are gone. I wiped out any credit I had, borrowed money from any place I could get it, and it's never enough."

"But you maintained the insurance policy on the land. You told me yesterday." Brody couldn't help the spark of anger burning in his core at the almost emotionless way Greg recounted burning down his own family's property. There had to have been another way, a better recourse, a solution which didn't include breaking the law.

"I know. Dad couldn't. Living on their savings and Social Security wasn't cutting it. Medicare covers a lot, but not everything. The condo they're renting wasn't gonna let them go another month without some kind of assurance they'd make the rent. Mom's worsened enough the doctors are mentioning hospice care. Dad's at his wit's end, and I'm the only one he could turn to."

"Start with the fires, Greg? More than one?"

He nodded, his head hung in shame. "I knew if the family property was the only thing destroyed, me and my family would be the first suspects. Heck, the only suspects. So, I burned down that derelict shack, the one off Cumberland. Place was practically falling down anyway. Nobody around who'd care what happened to it. I waited a couple of weeks, then did it again. Figured I'd establish a pattern. After the first two fires, once things quieted down, I torched the barn." He raised a pleading gaze to Brody. "I'm sorry. You have no idea how much I hate putting you in a position to deal with my actions, but I couldn't see another way out."

"I get it. Nobody suspected you, since you had no ties to the first fires. So when it happened on your family's land, nothing would point to you or your dad."

"Exactly. When you called, and told me you suspected arson, I lost it. You and Rafe, you're smart. You're thorough. I knew it was only a matter of time until you figured it out. But I hoped if I could destroy any evidence before you'd have a chance to look too close, maybe, I don't know— things could have turned out different."

"Greg, evidence was collected immediately after the fire. It had already been turned in to the forensic laboratory. Photographs were taken at the scene. A thorough investigation was underway before you torched what little remained of the barn. All you did was reinforce what we already knew, it was arson." Brody turned in his chair, watching his childhood friend, head bowed, eyes downcast. It couldn't be helped, Greg was in a butt load of trouble, looking at some serious time behind bars, and as much as he wanted to help him, he didn't have a whole lot of options.

"Setting the second fire simply raised my suspicions. You panicked, didn't you? That's why you showed up in Shiloh Springs. You wanted to know what I'd found."

Greg nodded. "I couldn't stand the not knowing. Sitting and waiting for the other shoe to drop, you know. It was stupid, but I figured I'd be able to read you. When we were growing up, you were like an open book. But you've changed."

"I'm not the only one who changed, Greg."

Brody turned away from Greg, turning his attention to his brother. "Rafe, I heard back from the forensic lab in Austin. They confirmed arson. Gasoline was the accelerant. They passed along the pieces of glass found at the scene, and found two usable fingerprints. Both belong to Greg."

He ignored Greg's barely audible gasp, pulled up the reports on his cell phone and passed it to his brother.

"Greg, you've admitted to starting at least four fires."

"Five."

Brody's head whipped around. "Five?" A horrible thought popped into his head. "Santiago's last night? That was you?"

"Yeah. After I got home, my girlfriend confronted me. She'd heard your messages on the answering machine, and demanded to know if I knew anything about the fire. I lied, told her I didn't have any idea who'd set the fire at the barn, like I lied to you. But the more I thought about it, I knew you were closing in. I figured if I could distract you, turn your attention in another direction, I'd buy some time to figure a way out."

"Greg, have you submitted a claim to the insurance company for the barn?" Rafe leaned back in his chair, with a subtle glance at the recorder, still taping Greg's confession.

"What? No!"

"Why not? After all, that was the point of this whole fiasco, wasn't it?" Brody couldn't quite keep the edge out of his question, cutting off the flow of words before he lost his composure. He needed to stay professional and not let the whole situation become personal. Because it felt personal.

"I...I thought I'd better wait. You know, until the property was released. Honestly, I was too scared to file. How stupid is that? I did this to get the insurance money, and then didn't even ask for it. What can I say, I'm a moron."

Brody leaned forward, forcing Greg to meet his stare. "Did your mom or dad know what you planned? Did they ask you to set the fire, hoping for the insurance payout?"

"No! Brody, I swear they don't know anything. They don't even know about the insurance policy being continued."

"Are you sure? Because I checked with the carrier, and they said they sent the renewal notice for the recent policy to the address in Florida."

Greg's eyes widened even as he shook his head vehemently. "That's not possible. They mail everything to me in San Antonio. I've got all the paperwork, the policy information. It's all at my place. As far as my parents know, the policy lapsed over two years ago. This is all on me, Brody."

Brody leaned back. He'd been bluffing, hoping to catch Greg in a lie, glad the Summers weren't involved. That would have been a blow not only to his dad and momma, but for all the people in Shiloh Springs who liked and respected the Summers. It was going to be hard enough when they found out about Greg's involvement.

"Talk to me about the fires. Take me through how you did it."

"All of them, or just the barn?"

"I know how the first two were started, so skip those. How'd you burn the barn down?"

Greg scrubbed his hands across his face, then rubbed his bloodshot eyes. He looked like he hadn't slept in days. "You know about the gasoline. I bought it on my way from San Antonio. Filled a container. I had a lot of old beer bottles and some old towels. Made homemade Molotov cocktails. I wiped down the bottles before I filled them. I bought some disposable gloves, but I guess I wasn't careful enough, if you found prints."

Rafe placed a bottle of water in front of Greg, who twisted off the cap and guzzled it down before continuing.

"Honestly, after the first two, I thought it would be easier to torch the barn. But it wasn't, it was ten times harder. I tossed in the first bottle, and the fire refused to catch. Can you believe it? I waited and waited, and nothing. Finally, I tossed in another one, aiming for the wall, and it caught. I used a total of six." Greg stared off in the distance, as if reliving the moment. "It was oddly beautiful, the flames shooting upward. The colors seemed more vivid, vibrant against the darkness. An ethereal beauty in its simplicity. The fire seemed to dance, sinuous and exotic, shooting sparks. It seemed alive, with a voracious appetite, consuming the building, yet leaving the surrounding area untouched. Like it had a mind of its own and once satisfied, dissipated and disappeared."

"Tell me about last night. Why burn Santiago's restaurant?"

"I told you, it was a distraction, to get your attention off our place. If you were focused on putting out the fire there, investigating it, you'd stop looking into a simple old barn fire that didn't hurt anybody."

Brody shook his head. "That's not how it works, Greg. All you've done is dig an even bigger hole to bury yourself in. The evidence is mounting."

"You won't need the evidence. I confess. I'll plead guilty, as long as you keep my folks out of this."

"You know the insurance company won't pay out for arson, don't you, Greg? Your parents won't see a dime. You did all of this for nothing." Rafe stood and pushed the button on the recorder, shutting it off. "I'm sorry about your mother."

Greg hung his head, hands twisted in his lap. "Yeah, me too. I did it all for them."

Brody stood and laid his hand on Greg's shoulder. "Rafe, place him under arrest. I'll contact the Texas Department of Public Safety and let them know he's been apprehended and confessed to multiple arsons."

With a heavy heart, Brody walked out of Rafe's office, as Rafe led Greg to an awaiting empty cell. Case solved. So why did the resolution leave him feeling gut punched and sad?

"Brody, wait!" Sally Anne clamored from behind her desk, blocking him from exiting the building.

"Not now. I've got to—"

"You've got to head to your parents' house stat. Nica called. Jamie's missing."

CHAPTER TWENTY-ONE

B eth raced through the front door of the Big House, out of breath, Camilla close on her heels. Nica stood in the hall, phone to her ear. She held up her hand, and continued her conversation, her voice low, almost a whisper. Beth wanted to shake her, scream at the top of her lungs for her baby. Instead, she sprinted past Nica, headed up the stairs. Maybe Jamie was hiding, thinking everything was a big game. She threw open every closed door, calling out her daughter's name at every single one.

Camilla stayed mere steps behind, arms wrapped across her middle, her face pale and drawn. She looked guilty, and even though Beth wanted to hug her and tell her it wasn't her fault, she couldn't stop. Jamie was missing.

"I've called Momma and Dad, they're on their way. Heath's heading for town, but he's keeping his eyes open. Brody's in a meeting with Rafe, and can't be disturbed. Sally Anne said she'll tell them as soon as they're free. I'm alerting the rest of the posse. We'll find her."

Beth slumped down onto the edge of somebody's bed, she wasn't sure whose. "What happened? Everything was fine when I left."

"She was playing upstairs. Drawing and coloring a picture for Uncle Brody, that's what she said. I went outside to chase down Otto. He got out of his pen again. I swear he's Houdini reincarnated. I wasn't gone more than five, ten minutes tops. When I came back in, I grabbed some stuff from the fridge, figured I'd whip up sandwiches for everybody for lunch. I thought Jamie might like to help, and came upstairs to get her. Only she wasn't here."

"You didn't see anything?"

Nica shook her head. "I'm sorry. I never should have left the house. I thought—I don't know what I thought. I'm an idiot."

"Evan couldn't have gotten onto the property. He doesn't even know we're here."

"Could somebody in town have told him? If they thought he was a stranger looking for directions?" Camilla sat on the bed beside Beth, and slung her arm around her shoulder. "He's clever enough to try something like that."

"I guess it's possible. Somebody might not have seen his picture broadcast all over the TV." Beth jumped up, heading for the door. "I can't just sit here doing nothing."

"You can't leave, not until Brody or Rafe gets here."

"I'm going to check the barn. She might be there."

"I already looked there." Nica trailed along behind Beth. "She wasn't there."

Beth never stopped walking. "Well, I can check it again."

"Right, good plan. Let's check the barn." Nica lunged around Beth, and opened the kitchen door, holding it while Beth and Camilla walked through. "I've also called Dane, and he's riding in from the pasture. He's keeping his eyes peeled, in case she wandered farther than she'd intended."

Beth broke into a sprint, reaching the barn before the other two women, and flung open the open. No easy feat, but she felt supercharged, hellbent on finding her child. The barn cat snuggled on an old blanket, the tiny kittens nuzzled against her, feeding. She explored every nook and cranny, looking into stalls, even behind stacks of hay. No Jamie.

"Gimme a second, let me look up there." Nica started climbing the wooden ladder leading to the barn's upper level.

"Jamie knows she's not allowed up there."

"She's a kid. Kids love to go places where they're not supposed to. It's part of growing up." Nica scampered up the rest of the way to the loft, her head raised high enough she could spy the entire loft area. Beth's heart sank when Nica shook her head, and started climbing down.

"Where is she? I swear if Evan has her, I'm going to kill him."

Camilla snorted. "Get in line, girlfriend."

Beth spun around and raced outside at the sound of her name being called. Brody was here! He'd find Jamie.

"Brody!" She flung herself into his arms, her whole body trembling. Strong arms encircled her, pulling her against his warmth. Taking a deep breath, she fought back tears. Now wasn't the time to fall apart, that could come later. Right now, she needed to be the fierce warrior he'd claimed, and move heaven and earth to find her child.

"What happened?"

"Jamie's missing. I'd gone to see Camilla at Dane's house. Nica was keeping an eye on Jamie. She called me, told me Jamie's gone. Have you heard anything about Evan? Is he here? Could he have my baby?"

"Calm down. Nobody's seen or heard anything about your ex. Nothing new, anyway. We'll find her, I promise." Brody's hand cupped the back of her head, and she leaned back, staring into his eyes, and read his determination and promise.

"I know."

Brody's arm snaked around her waist at the sound of a car speeding toward the house from the front gate, followed by a second. Rafe's truck screeched to a stop, and he jumped out, jogging toward Brody and Beth. Ms. Patti's white Cadillac Escalade rocked to a stop beside Rafe's truck. Looked like Nica's call about rounding up the posse worked, because people suddenly seemed to be coming out of the woodwork.

"Any word?" Brody asked as soon as Rafe was within speaking distance.

"Remember I told you about the woman's car being stolen at Beth's old apartment complex? Turns out her cell phone is missing, too. She thinks it might still be in the car."

"Can you trace it somehow?" A tiny speck of hope blossomed inside Beth, despite knowing the chances of the woman's phone being anywhere near Evan were slim to none. A slim chance was more than she'd had a few minutes ago.

"Chance hauled his backside over to Judge Jenkins' house with a warrant. We've got also got the owner's permission. I've already called the phone carrier and alerted them a warrant is coming, and they're ready to go the second we've got the judge's signature. Fingers crossed the phone is inside the stolen car and Stewart hasn't spotted it and tossed it."

"But we don't know he's got Jamie."

"True." Rafe studied Beth's face, and there was something indefinable in his eyes. He was hiding something, she could feel it."

"What aren't you telling me, Rafe?"

He shook his head. "We need to search every place. Let's round up everybody, and we'll start doing a grid pattern search. Maybe she got lost, and can't find her way back to the house. She's not familiar with all of the property. Maybe she wandered a little too far, and we'll find her."

"We've searched everywhere in the house, Rafe," Nica spoke up. "I even looked in the attic, in case she got bored and went exploring." She slapped her hands across her mouth, her eyes glazed with tears. "It's my fault. I was supposed to be watching her. Instead I went chasing after that stupid donkey. If anything happens to her…"

"Jamie's gonna be fine. Nobody wants to hurt her. Even if Stewart somehow got hold of her, the man is her father. He won't hurt her."

Ms. Patti stepped into the center of the gathered family. "Rafe's right. Let's regroup, see who's here, and get everybody looking for Jamie." Beth listened as Ms. Patti started listing off everybody. "Heath's covering the road into town, doing a slow sweep. Dusty and Sally Anne have set up a command center at the sheriff's office. Antonio's on his way with Serena and Tessa. They should be here within the next fifteen minutes. Nica, Camilla, and Beth already started the search of the house. Dane's riding in, should be—there he is," Ms. Patti gestured toward a lone man on horseback, riding at a fast clip toward them.

"Dad's out on a job site with Liam. I talked to Liam, and they'll be on their way ASAP." Brody pulled Beth closer against his side, and Beth couldn't help feeling a little bit better. He was her rock, her stability, her safe place, and once they found Jamie, she was going to tell him how she felt. Who cared they hadn't had the traditional courtship with all the trappings? Her feelings were real and they were true. Brody had become her friend in the beginning, and every time she'd been around him, gotten to know him a little better, her feelings changed. Became more. She loved him with all her heart, and maybe, if she was really lucky, he felt the same about her.

"We've checked the house and the barn." Beth turned to Brody. "What should we do next?"

Before he answered, Rafe's phone rang, and he answered on the first ring. "Boudreau."

He listened, gave a brief nod to Brody, and hung up. "We've got the warrant. Chance made the call to the phone company, and they are pinging cell towers, trying to triangulate a location." Turning to the assembled crowd, he barked orders, handing out assignments.

"Nica, Camilla, you stay close to the house in case Jamie shows up. Beth, go with them."

"But—"

"No buts. When Jamie's found, she's going to need her mother. Some place where she'll feel safe."

"I understand." She'd do anything Rafe asked, if it meant holding her baby in her arms again.

"Momma, check around your gazebo, see if Jamie found it and she's playing there."

Without a word, Ms. Patti disappeared around the side of the house. Beth pictured the magical gazebo Brody had shown her in its fairy tale setting, and hoped Jaime somehow found it and was playing inside, not realizing the worry she'd caused everyone.

"Dane, since you're already saddled up, ride the tree line behind the house and to the east, see if you spot anything. Brody and I will walk the supply trail behind the barn area. Keep your phones handy. Don't hesitate to shout out if—

when—you find something."

Beth followed Nica and Camilla into the house, but couldn't stay still. She paced the living room, wearing a rut in the area rug. Arms wrapped across her middle, she jumped at every noise. Standing in the living room, she looked at everything, yet saw nothing except her baby's face in her mind. Jamie, when she'd been born, screeching at the top of her lungs, with her squished red face, counting all her tiny fingers and toes. Jamie, smiling at her as her front teeth came in, drool running down her chin. Jamie, when she'd taken her first steps. She'd barely crawled, simply pulling herself upright and going from standing to racing in no time. Or her second birthday when she'd blown out all the candles, and covered the cake with slobber. Nobody cared, they'd simply scraped off the frosting and celebrated.

Nica knelt beside her and wrapped her arms around Beth, rocking her gently. She hadn't even realized she'd fallen to her knees in the middle of the rug until then.

"It's going to be alright, Beth. We'll find her. She can't have gone too far. Bet she'll come racing in, like nothing even happened. Wait and see."

"She's so little, and she's never wandered off before." Beth looked into Nica's eyes, despair crowding out the fear. "He's got my baby. Somehow, he found out we were here, and he's taken her."

"Beth, don't think like that. You don't know your ex has her. I'm not gonna lie to you, it's a possibility. A slim one, but I'm not going to try and sugarcoat things. You're a strong woman, and Jamie's going to need you to be strong, because when she comes home, she is going to need her mother."

"I swear, if Evan has taken her, I'm going to kill him."

Nica barked out a broken laugh. "Don't say that in front of Rafe, because he's the law, but if Evan took her, I'll give you the gun."

Beth wiped at her eyes, determined not to cry. There'd be time for tears later. Right now, she needed to be calm. Be strong. For Jamie.

"I can't stay here, doing nothing. Where else can we look? I know Rafe said not to leave the house, so let's look here. Start going room by room."

Nica stood and extended her hand to Beth. "Let's start at the top and work our way down. I already checked the attic, but let's look again."

Beth took her hand, letting the younger woman help her to her feet. "Let's find my daughter."

CHAPTER TWENTY-TWO

Lady Luck was on his side today. First, he'd gotten the info of where Beth was hiding. He wasn't surprised she was shacking up with one of the lousy Boudreaus, but then again, Beth was an opportunist, and beautiful to boot. She'd managed to twist him around her little finger at the beginning of their relationship too. Why wouldn't she do it to another man? She'd use him and abuse him, toss him out like yesterday's trash the minute she found something bigger and better.

Evan's luck continued when he'd found an isolated road, practically depositing him on the Boudreaus' back doorstep. It looked like something used for loading and hauling ranching stuff. He didn't care; it worked for his purpose, an unobserved spot to stay out of sight and provide a quick getaway if he was spotted. Dame Fortune continued shining down on him when he'd spotted Jamie from his hiding place, skipping out the back door, headed toward the barn. After that, it had been too easy.

"Daddy, you promised Mommy could come with us to get ice cream."

Evan rolled his eyes at Jamie's words. She hadn't shut up from the minute she gotten in the car. When she'd spotted him in the trees, crouching hidden out of sight from those nosy Boudreaus, she'd raced across the grass, flinging herself into his arms. It was a true miracle nobody spotted her, practically doing cartwheels on her way toward his hiding place. He'd squeezed her tight, felt her tears against the skin of his neck as she blubbered about how much she'd missed him, and why had he stayed gone so long. Apparently, that was one thing in Beth's favor—she hadn't told the brat about him being behind bars. He'd love to know what story she'd concocted for Jamie about his long absence.

"I'll call her again in a little while, okay? She can meet us and we'll go get your ice cream."

"We have to go back, Daddy. I'm supposed to help take care of the kitties. The mommy cat had babies!"

"Kitties—you mean kittens? Why should you take care of them? Don't they have people to do that?"

Jamie squirmed around in the back seat, wiggling as much as the seatbelt allowed. "I like playing with the kitties. They're little, and they squirm a lot when I pick them up, and they kiss me all over my face. And I get to chase them. It's fun."

"Later, Jamie. You can play with them later."

"Where are we going? I'm not supposed to go any place without Mommy. I don't want her to get mad at me. Maybe you should call her again."

It's okay. I'll let Mommy know where you are, baby. We're going to stop in a minute, and I'll call her." *Does this child ever stop talking?*

"Did you know I got to play with Otto?"

"Who's Otto? Does he work for the Boudreaus?" Evan maneuvered around a slow-moving truck pulling a trailer. Something inside reeked, and he held his breath. The stench was enough to bring tears to his eyes. How could people stand living with the stench? He punched the accelerator, speeding away from the truck, continuing north and east. According to his map, it shouldn't be too much farther until he hit one of the big interstates. He'd have a much better chance of putting some distance between him and Shiloh Springs once he hit civilization again.

"Daddy, is it time to call Mommy yet? She's gonna be really mad at me. I wasn't supposed to leave." Jamie's voice quieted, and he could barely hear her. "I disobeyed her, and went outside even though she told me to stay in the house. I wanted to see the kitties, but Nica told me to wait and she'd go with me, but she had to chase Otto. That was funny. I think Otto was laughing at her."

Right, Otto the donkey.

A convenience store loomed up ahead in the distance, and within a few minutes, Evan pulled into the parking lot, easing the car around the side where no other cars parked. Jamie's eyes darted around, taking in everything, but at least she'd stopped talking for the first time since she'd gotten in the car. He'd never realized how much the brat droned on and on. Then again, he'd stayed gone as much as humanly possible, so this might actually be normal behavior for her.

It was now or never. If he made the call, the state would tack on a half dozen or more charges to his record, including kidnapping, felony escape, and a laundry list of foul deeds. Didn't matter the brat was his, he was an escaped convict, no longer a custodial parent. He shook his head. Why was he even debating the situation? His path was set the second he'd climbed in the back of Axel's girlfriend's car. No turning back.

Reaching onto the front seat, he picked up the cell phone and dialed. He'd been fortunate when he'd picked this car to steal. The owner's cell phone must've slid out of her purse and wedged between the seats when she'd gotten out and got the groceries. He'd only found it when it rang. Scared the spit out of him, before he realized what it was. So, he had wheels and a means of communication. And now he had a hostage—his own daughter.

Steeling his nerves, he dialed Beth's number. He knew she had the same cell number she'd had when they were married. His attorney had listed it on some papers in his briefcase, and Evan had spotted it, making a mental note.

He said a silent prayer Beth would cooperate—because there was no turning back now.

Beth jumped when her phone rang, and she snatched it from her jeans pocket, and answered, not even bothering to look at the caller ID.

"Mommy!"

"Baby, where are you? I've been so worried."

"We're going for ice cream. Daddy said it was okay, because he hadn't seen me in a long time, and he wanted us to have a special treat. Are you coming, Mommy?"

A cold sweat broke out across her skin at her daughter's words. Evan had Jamie! Her worst nightmare had come true. She watched Nica motioning wildly, trying to get her attention, but Beth ignored her, focusing all her concentration on her daughter.

"Of course! I want to have ice cream too, sweetie. Where are you? I'll come meet you."

"Um, I'm not sure, Mommy. It looks like—"

"Hello, Beth." Evan's voice was devoid of any emotion, monotone and cold.

"Where's my daughter?"

"Our daughter."

"You have no rights to Jamie. You signed the custody agreement voluntarily when you went to prison, remember. You relinquished all parental rights without a single regret. Those were your words, Evan. Remember? Just tell me what you want."

"What do you think I want, Beth? I want what I should have had from the very beginning. Money. I worked hard for it. I'm the one who did all the research. I'm the one who figured out the bond was still valid. I'm the one who realized its true worth. I deserve every penny, and I intend to get what's coming to me."

"Oh, trust me, Evan, I'll make sure you get everything coming to you."

"Daddy, I think I want to go home now. We don't need ice cream. I wanna see Mommy." The confusion and fear in Jamie's voice sent Beth to her knees. Her precious baby, in the hands of the man who'd tried to murder her sister, and had planned Beth's own demise, had her daughter.

Muffled in the background, she heard the sound of footsteps racing inside the house from outside, but refused to focus on anything but the phone plastered against her ear. The dead silence on the other end terrified her.

"Jamie, sweetheart, can you hear me?"

"She's fine. I haven't hurt a single hair on her head, and I won't if you do what I tell you."

"Evan, so help me, I'm going to rip your eyes out with my bare hands. Give me back my daughter."

"I want my money."

"I don't have it. Every dime went back to the county. You know Tessa and I donated the bond back to Crowley County. And you, you left me in debt up to my eyeballs. Mortgages on the house. Credit cards in my name I didn't open. Bank accounts empty. Even Jamie's college fund's gone. What more do you want from me?"

Brody knelt in front of her, his eyes searching her face. With his finger pressed to his lips, he mouthed the word, "speaker." When she stared at him blankly, he eased the phone away from her ear and tapped a button, putting the phone on speaker.

"You better figure out a way to get your hands on some cash fast, Beth, if you want me out of your life for good. I don't intend to spend another day in prison."

"How much do you want, Evan?"

"A million dollars." Though his answer didn't surprise her, the amount still had her heart rate kicking into high gear, and her breath caught.

"I don't have a million dollars. Where do you think I can come up with that kind of money, Evan?"

"I'll pay it."

The strong, deep voice from behind Beth had her head whipping around, and she stared into the eyes of Douglas Boudreau, her mouth open in surprise. "Douglas?"

"Who's there?"

"Douglas Boudreau. I can get your money. No cash though, not on a Sunday. No banks are open."

Evan's surprised curse was clear through the receiver.

"Daddy, you said bad words. Mommy doesn't like bad words. She says they're in-a-something." Beth bit back a strangled laugh at her daughter's admonition. Jamie had picked up a couple of not-so-nice cuss words around some of the hands since being at the ranch, when they hadn't known she was around. More than once Beth had to talk to her about their inappropriateness. Guess she was rubbing off on her daughter.

"Douglas Boudreau? The one who owns the construction company, right?" Evan's chuckle was pure evil. A shiver ran down Beth's spine at the sound. "Don't worry, Mr. Boudreau, I wouldn't expect you to have a million dollars in cash laying around. Then again, I don't know anything about most of you Boudreaus, though I've met two of your sons."

"Get to the point, Mr. Stewart. The sooner we do this, the sooner Jamie can be back with her mother." Beth had never heard Douglas' voice sound so—commanding. Without conscious thought, she found herself standing straighter, almost at attention, before she caught herself. Brody mentioned his father had been in the Army, something to do with Special Forces, but with everything going on, she'd forgotten that fact. Now his superior training was evident within every syllable the older man spoke. He'd taken control of the situation, letting Evan know he no longer had the upper hand.

"The point, Mr. Boudreau, is simple. Money. This transaction can be accomplished simply and efficiently, with nobody getting hurt."

"Before I give you one single penny, Jamie will be returned to her mother. No exception."

"I can't do that. How do I know you'll fulfill your end of the bargain if I give you my only bargaining chip?"

"Because you'll have me in Jamie's place. Trust me, I've worth far more than your daughter, Stewart. You said you know who I am. Then you'll also know I'm a man of my word. Trade Jamie for me, and you'll get exactly what's coming to you."

There was silence, Beth's nerves tight, her body on edge, waiting for Evan's answer. She didn't want Douglas putting himself in Jamie's place, but her daughter was so little. She didn't understand what a monster her father had become, and she was terrified of what Evan might do if his demands were thwarted.

"I agree to your terms, Mr. Boudreau."

Beth's body collapsed into Brody's arms, relief swamping her. Her baby was coming home. Things weren't settled yet, not by a long shot, but they were one step closer to ending Evan's reign of terror. Because she knew Brody wouldn't allow Evan to walk away from this unscathed. He'd make sure Evan ended back behind bars. And he'd have backup, because he had his family to watch his back.

"Where do you want to make the exchange?" Douglas glanced toward Beth, his gaze steady and reassuring. He gave a brief nod in her direction before turning his attention back to Evan.

"I'll call you back in an hour. There are arrangements that need to be in place before I'll meet you. Be ready."

"Evan, let me talk to Jamie. Please." Beth pulled herself out of Brody's arms and raced over to stand by Douglas, her eyes glued to the cell phone. "Please," she choked out again.

For another long stretch, there was silence, and she wondered if he'd let her speak to their daughter. Putting herself in Jamie's place, she knew her baby had to be terrified. Evan was her father, but she hadn't been around him in months. And now she knew her ex's true colors, leaving Jamie with him for even a minute seemed an eternity.

"Mommy! Where are you? Daddy said you were gonna have ice cream with us, but then you never came. Now I want to come home, and Daddy said no."

"Hey, baby girl! We'll have ice cream soon, I promise. We're going to come and get you, and you'll be home soon. Then you can eat anything you want, okay?"

"Anything?"

"I promise. Just be a good girl until we get there. You can do that, right?"

Beth fervently wished this was a video call, so she could see her daughter's face. She sounded unharmed, unfazed by the drama of what was going on around here, but how long would that last?

"Can you hurry up, Mommy? I don't like this car. It smells funny." Her voice lowered into a whisper, "And Daddy's being mean. I want to come home."

Tears spilled down Beth's cheeks, and she felt Brody's arms slide around her waist, felt the warmth and safety of being within his arms. She shook her head, trying to speak but unable to get the words to come.

"Honey bear, we'll be there soon. Ms. Patti will fix you some frozen waffles and we'll put ice cream and chocolate syrup on them. Even whipped cream. How's that sound?"

"Uncle Brody! Are you coming to get me?"

"Absolutely."

"Enough." Evan's voice came through the phone. "I'll call you with instructions, and make sure you bring a laptop, Mr. Boudreau." With that, the call ended.

Pandemonium ensued the second the call stopped. Everyone was talking at once, and Beth couldn't follow a single conversation, all her thoughts focused on Jamie. She spun around to face Douglas.

"Thank you. I'll figure out a way to pay you back."

Douglas reached forward and took her hand, squeezing it gently. "Darlin', you're part of this family now. Not like I'm going to let somebody like Evan Stewart get away with hurting you or Jamie. Don't worry about the money, Jamie's the most important thing, and we're gonna get her back. She'll be in your arms in no time."

"I'm going with you." Brody's voice was a simple statement of fact, but she heard the underlying steel layering each word. "I promised her I'd be there, and I'm going."

"Me, too."

"Beth—"

"You're not going to talk me out of coming, Brody. She's my daughter!"

"And what's to stop Evan from trying to grab you too,

and take you both out of the country?" She could almost hear his unspoken *or worse.*

"You are." She cupped his cheek, gazing into his brown eyes. "You and Douglas and Rafe and whoever else you drag into your rescue plan. I know we're your first priority."

"My only priority."

Glancing around, she noted they were the only two people still standing in the living room. Everyone else had cleared out, giving them the illusion of privacy, though knowing her sister, she probably had her ear pressed to the opening of the kitchen, listening to every word.

"Go. I know your dad, Rafe, and the others are meeting someplace, coming up with a plan to capture Evan and rescue Jamie. Help them. But know this, I'm going with you. If you try to stop me, I'll simply follow you."

He chuckled. "I know you would." Brushing a soft kiss against her forehead, he turned her toward the kitchen, giving her a nudge. "Go talk to your sister. I'll be back."

Taking a deep breath, she headed for the kitchen, the heart of the Boudreau home, and prayed like she'd never prayed before her baby stayed safe, and Brody didn't end up killing Evan.

CHAPTER TWENTY-THREE

In under an hour, Evan called back with instructions. Brody and the others had put contingencies into place, calling in favors throughout the surrounding counties, making sure all their bases were covered, regardless of where Evan wanted to do the exchange. He still couldn't believe his dad offered himself in exchange for Jamie. Not that he was surprised by his dad's act, but that he'd beat him to the punch. All along, he'd intended to offer himself in exchange for sweet little Jamie, knowing Evan held a grudge against him for being part of his arrest.

Evan made sure the meet-up took place outside of Shiloh Springs County, so Rafe's jurisdiction was limited—or so he thought. Idiot didn't realize the Boudreaus had friends in almost every branch of law enforcement, and didn't mind calling in markers owed. Now the State Highway Patrol, Texas Rangers, FBI, and a host of local jurisdictions were all on the lookout for the stolen car, Evan, and Jamie.

Evan's demands were simple. Douglas was to come alone, with his laptop, and the cell phone. Demanded he drive toward Williamson County, get on Interstate 45, and head north toward Dallas. Then he'd text further instructions.

Traffic was light, since it was late on a Sunday, but that didn't mean there wasn't still spots of congestion. This was Texas; there was *always* construction on their highways and interstates. Rafe and Brody followed their dad's truck, staying at least thirty yards behind, but close enough they could spot trouble. They'd been on I-45 for about fifteen minutes or so when Douglas' truck slowed perceptibly. His blinker indicated he was taking the next exit. They were still inside Williamson County.

Brody's hands tightened on the wheel, while Rafe called his contact with the Williamson's Sheriff's Department, relaying the exit number. His heartbeat kicked up a notch, and he kept his eyes glued to his dad's taillights. He drove within the posted speed limits, though he doubted anybody would pull him over. Every available cop was watching, monitoring the situation, but keeping a respectful distance. Nobody wanted things to go south, not with a child involved.

The blinker on his dad's truck clicked on, indicating a left turn, and Brody eased into the left lane. A quick glance at Rafe showed his brother's whole body tensed for action, ready to spring at a moment's notice. This was happening— soon. He could feel it in his gut, that feeling of everything slowing down around him, coming into sharp focus. It was the same feeling he got when he was fighting a fire. He knew every movement, every nuance of what the flames would do, and he was prepared and ready to fight it, tame it, control it. And he'd do the same here with Evan.

"Be ready," he said, tightening his grip on the wheel.

"I've got this. Don't go off half-cocked. We have to stay outta sight, or Stewart's gonna try to run. I wouldn't put it past him to use Jamie as a human shield."

His father's truck made a right turn into a Braum's parking lot, and Rafe pointed toward the stolen car, and then toward the inside of the ice cream store. Stewart sat at one of the little tables with Jamie, a cup of ice cream sitting in front of her. He continued through the parking lot toward a sandwich shop a couple of storefronts over, and parked in front of it. Douglas climbed out of his car, and headed inside, straight for Evan's table.

"Here we go." Rafe laid his cell phone on his lap. Douglas had the cell phone Evan gave him in his hand, but his personal cell was in his jacket pocket, already on speaker. Their end was muted, so Evan wouldn't accidentally hear anything from their end, but they'd be able to hear every word. Antonio had wanted to wire Douglas, but everyone agreed Evan might ask Douglas to prove he wasn't wearing a wire. This was their next best option on such short notice.

"Hey, Jamie." Douglas squatted down beside her, ruffling his hand through her hair, and Brody felt a clenching sensation in the middle of his chest. He adored that little girl. If anything happened to her, he'd never forgive himself.

"Mr. Douglas!" Jamie wrapped her arms around Douglas' neck. "Did you come to take me home? I wanna see Mommy."

"You're gonna be going home in a minute, sweet pea. I need to talk to your daddy for a few minutes, okay?" He pointed to a table beside the one where Evan and Douglas were sitting. "It's grown-up talk, so we're going to sit right over here. You eat your ice cream."

"We can stay right here," Evan started saying, but Douglas cut him off.

"She doesn't need to hear this. She'll be fine, right where she is. You'll be watching her the entire time. Not like I'm going to try to pull anything. Not while you're holding all the cards."

"Fine. Where's your laptop?" Evan scowled clear enough Brody could see it through the plate glass window. "You need to wire the money into my account."

"Not until Jamie is safe and away from all this. That was the deal."

"Deals change. You wire the money first."

"Not gonna happen, Stewart. You want the million, Jamie goes free."

Evan's eyes widened and he looked around frantically. "I told you to come alone!"

"Calm down. I didn't bring anybody. I followed your instructions to the letter. I can call my son, and he'll come pick Jamie up and leave. Then you'll get your money. Plus,

I'll add in a bonus. I've got a private plane on speed dial. It's already fueled and waiting. Twenty minutes away from here, with a pilot standing by. He'll fly you anywhere you want to go, no strings attached. Think about it, Stewart. Your only problem will be deciding where you want to spend your million dollars."

Brody choked on the breath he'd been holding. What game was his father playing? They didn't have a plane, much less one on standby. He looked at Rafe, who shrugged. Guess he was clueless, too.

"Which one?" Evan's voice came through the phone, drawing them back to the situation unfolding inside the ice cream shop.

"Which one what?"

"Which son are you going to call?"

"Does it matter?" Douglas' voice sounded so nonchalant, you'd never know the man was in the middle of a hostage situation involving a four-year-old little girl. His dad really had nerves of steel.

"Can't be that lousy sheriff. He'd try to pull a fast one, and take me in. I'm not going back to jail." Evan paused for a moment and then laughed, the sound sending a chill up Brody's spine. "Make it Brody. I heard he's been sniffing around my wife. Maybe we should have a little chat before I leave the country. Besides, I owe him for pulling a shotgun on me."

Douglas held up the cell phone not currently in use,

wiggling it in front of Evan. "I'm going to call him now. I'll put it on speaker so you can hear the whole thing, and know this isn't a set-up. I simply want Jamie safe and returned to her mother."

"Call him, but no funny business, or me and the brat will be gone, and you'll never find us, I swear."

The phone rang, and Brody answered on the first ring. "Dad, what's happening? Did you find Stewart? Is Jamie okay?"

"Everything's fine. I'm with them now. Jamie's eating ice cream, and Stewart and I have come to an understanding. How far are you from Williamson County?"

"Roughly fifteen, maybe twenty minutes."

"Head up the interstate north. I'll text you directions. Follow them exactly."

"Tell him not to bring anybody with him, or we're outta here."

"I know what to do. Dad, be careful, I don't trust Stewart."

He heard Stewart's bark of laughter. "Like I trust you, either."

Brody ignored the other man's taunt. "I'll be there as fast as I can, Dad."

He disconnected the line, turning to Rafe. "Alright, here's what I think we should do." Ignoring his brother's smirk, he continued, "You head to the back door, and see if you can get in the employee loading area. That way, you're inside in case things turn ugly. I'll pull around the building and come in from the street side, so Stewart doesn't know we're already here. Once I've got Jamie clear of the building, you and Dad take Stewart down."

He watched Rafe's face as he mulled over the plan. "I think it'll work. Drop me off around back, and make sure I get inside before you pull off."

Brody started the car and drove around the small row of shops, and pulled to a stop behind the Braum's. Before getting out of the car, Rafe unbuckled his ankle holster and handed it to Brody. "Just in case."

Brody silently eyed the gun before reluctantly taking it. "I don't want to use this."

"I know, but I don't trust Stewart not to try and pull a fast one. Once you have Jamie, take her to Beth." He knew Beth was spitting mad, because he'd refused to let her come with them. Arrangements had been made for her to be with Antonio. They were only a couple of blocks away, close enough to get Jamie to her within minutes, but far enough away she was out of the line of fire. Even though her anger had raked gouges in his soul, he'd refused to back down. There was nothing and nobody putting the woman he loved in danger.

"Everybody in place? You all heard the plan." Rafe spoke into the radio inside the unmarked car.

A string of affirmatives responded to his call. Everything was set. Rafe slid from the car and quickstepped to the rear door, knocking twice. It seemed like an eternity before a guy, little more than a kid really, answered. His eyes widened as big as saucers at whatever Rafe told him, but he opened the door and Brody watched Rafe ease inside, shooting him a thumb's up before disappearing.

The waiting seemed interminable; each minute of the clock seemed endless. He buckled the ankle holster in place, praying he wouldn't have to use Rafe's spare weapon. Once fifteen minutes passed, Brody pulled onto the street and then made a U-turn before heading into the parking lot, making it appear he'd come from the main road. He parked directly in front of the store, and stepped from the car, his hands spread at his side, so Stewart could see he wasn't holding anything.

The scent of grilled burgers and greasy fries hit him when he pulled the door open, his eyes darting back and forth between Stewart and his father. He hadn't taken more than two steps inside, when he was hit by three feet of flying blonde pigtails and two arms twined around his waist.

"Uncle Brody! You came, you came!"

"I promised you I'd come and get you, honey bear." He stared at Stewart, watching the other man, part of him hoping he'd get five minutes alone with him once the dust settled. The other half hoped the other man wasn't a complete idiot who'd escalate the situation. They didn't need any unnecessary bloodshed.

"Daddy and Mr. Douglas are here. They didn't want any ice cream. Did you want ice cream, Uncle Brody? I can share mine with you, but it's kinda melted."

"That's okay, honey bear. I don't need any ice cream right now." He ran a hand protectively over her back. "Dad, everything okay here?"

"It's good. You take Jamie and—"

"Not so fast, Boudreau. Brody, you take a seat with my daughter. Mr. Boudreau, Brody's staying put until you get your laptop. We have a transaction to make before anybody leaves."

"That wasn't the deal." Douglas argued.

"Deal's changed. Get the laptop." Stewart moved aside the flap of his button-front shirt, revealing the gun tucked into his waistband. "I suggest you move quickly."

Douglas clamored to his feet, and shot a look toward Brody. He nodded and led Jamie back to her table, hoping Rafe could see and hear what was happening. They'd only get one shot at this, and they'd need to take it soon.

Walking back in with a laptop computer, Douglas eased back onto the chair across from Stewart. "Did you check to see if this place has Wi-Fi? Otherwise, we're going to have to move to some place that does."

"They've got Wi-Fi. Here's the password." He slid a scrap of paper across the table. "Connect and let's get this over with. I want out of this lousy state.

Keeping his gaze on his father, he noted movement behind Stewart, who had kept his back to the kitchen and ice cream area, making sure he had a clear sight line through the front window. He spotted Rafe and a couple of other men inching closer to the small eat-in area.

"I've got a connection. Now let Brody and Jamie leave, and you'll get your blood money." Douglas held his hands over the keyboard, waiting.

"Right after you transfer the funds. I'm a reasonable man, Mr. Boudreau. But I'm not stupid. If I let Jamie go, I'll never see a dime of that money." Reaching into his pocket, he pulled out another ragged-edged paper. "Here's the account information and the routing number. Let's get this done, because I'm losing my patience."

Douglas lifted his hands from the keyboard, and crossed his arms over his chest. "No."

"What do you mean, no? We had a deal."

"Like you said, deal's changed. You want to change the rules partway through, fine. Now we'll do things my way. Brody, get Jamie out of here. Get in your car and drive away." He leaned back in his seat. "Unlike you, Mr. Stewart, I gave my word to exchange myself and the funds in exchange for Jamie. You wanted the money and a hostage. That's the deal. A plane and a full tank of gas, headed anywhere you want. An influential hostage. Nobody's going to try and stop you, not as long as you have me."

Stewart shot Brody a hate-filled glare. "Take her and get out!"

"Dad…"

"Everything's gonna be fine, Brody. Take Jamie to her

mother, where she belongs." Douglas held up his cell phone. "I'm making a call to the pilot, the second Jamie and Brody are out the door. Agreed?"

"Do it."

Brody lifted Jamie's trembling body into his arms and raced for the front door. During the exchange, Jamie had figured out something bad was happening, and her little body shook with fear. She buried her head into the crook of his neck, and he felt her warm tears against his skin. Throwing open the car door, he strapped her into the passenger seat, and ran around the car, sliding into the driver's seat. With a last look inside, he pulled away, tires squealing.

Jamie was safe. He'd left behind a disaster in the making, and he couldn't help wondering how they'd manage to disarm the situation, or if the only answer would be bloodshed.

CHAPTER TWENTY-FOUR

Beth lay beside Jamie. Her little girl slept after having been stuffed with waffles and whipped cream, and hugged by everyone within a five-mile radius. Now she was sleeping the sleep of the innocent. She'd loved being the center of attention, had chatted and preened as if nothing unusual happened, and fallen asleep almost the minute her head hit the pillow. Yet Beth couldn't seem to tear herself from Jamie's side. She hadn't let her out of her sight from the moment Brody slid Jamie into her arms.

She'd been furious with him, heck, with all the Boudreaus, for not allowing her to confront Evan. While mentally she knew everything worked out for the best, and they were right to keep her away, she still would have liked putting a bullet between Evan's eyes. On the bright side, he was back in custody, in solitary confinement, and he'd face enough charges to keep him there for the rest of his natural life. Couldn't happen to a better guy.

"How's she doing?" Brody leaned against the doorjamb, a smile touching his lips. His tender expression as he watched Jamie snuggle deeper into the blankets was filled with the love he felt for her little girl. He'd displayed it in so many ways, not the least of which was today's actions. There weren't many men who'd risk everything to rescue her child. But then again, there weren't many men like the Boudreau men.

"She's doing amazingly well, all things considered." Beth tucked the covers around Jamie tighter. She couldn't seem to stop touching her, making sure she was really here, and the nightmare was finally over.

"Move," she heard from the doorway, as Tessa shouldered her way past Brody. "Sis, you need to take a break. I'll sit with Jamie. Go get something to eat. Take a walk. She'll be here when you get back, I promise." Tessa made a shooing motion as she spoke. She grabbed Beth's hand and tugged her up, before taking her place on the bed.

"Are you sure?"

"I won't let her out of my sight. I'm going to sit right here until you come back." Tessa scooted up the bed until her back rested against the headboard. "Go, Jamie's fine."

Beth looked at Brody, who'd stood silently during her exchange with her sister. Without a word, he held out his hand, palm up. Without hesitating, she slid hers into his, feeling the warmth of his touch. Together, they walked down the stairs, and she stopped at the bottom, and closed her eyes.

"What's wrong?"

Opening her eyes, she smiled at Brody. "Nothing. For

the first time in a long time, everything is right. Evan can't hurt me or Jamie ever again. I'm…free."

"Beth, honey, can I fix you something to eat?" Ms. Patti's voice sounded from the kitchen, causing Beth to smile. She couldn't help but think about something her mother used to say. A true Southern woman fixes everything with food.

"No thanks, Ms. Patti. I think I'm gonna take a walk, clear my head."

"Alright, but be careful, it's dark out there."

"I'm going with her, Momma. She'll be fine." Brody gave her hand a squeeze when she tried to tug hers loose, and led her to the front door. Once on the front porch, she took a deep breath, feeling a sense of tranquility flood through her. She hadn't realized the effect Evan had on her life, even when he wasn't a daily part of it. Though they'd divorced after he went to prison, she'd never really believed he was truly out of her life for good.

"What's that smile for?"

"I realized I'm free. Free from Evan and his hold over my life. I guess I never truly let go of the specter he'd cast over me from the day we met. I feel like a giant weight has been lifted, and he can't touch me or Jamie ever again."

Releasing her hand, he cupped her face, tilting it up until she met his gaze. "I'm glad. You deserve every happiness life has to offer. I wish…"

"What?"

"I wish I'd met you before Evan. Before any of this happened. That I could have saved you from everything he's put you through. Seeing you smile—I can't explain how it makes me feel to know you're happy. I want to see you smile every day for the rest of your life."

"Brody, I—"

He pressed a fingertip against her lips. "Shh...let me finish. We're friends, Beth. I've felt a connection with you from the moment we met. Like an invisible thread, connecting us, pulling me closer and closer. It isn't like anything I've ever felt before, and I'll be honest, I fought against that pull because you weren't ready for anything more than friendship."

"I know." Her heartbeat stuttered inside her chest. He'd used the F word—friends. Was friendship all he wanted from her, all he could offer? The thought of losing Brody, of him not being part of her life, was breaking her heart. But if friendship was all he offered, she'd take it, because she couldn't imagine a day going by without talking to Brody. Not seeing him, knowing he'd be there for her—for Jamie— the thought was untenable.

"It didn't work. I can't walk away from this, from us. Beth, I love you. I think I've been in love with you from the beginning, but I held back because life had already thrown so many obstacles in your path, I didn't want to add one more if you didn't feel the same. Everything changed though, when your ex escaped. The thought of him laying a finger on you? I'm not running from my feelings anymore. I love you. I want to spend the rest of my life with you and Jamie, sharing everything. I can't promise there won't be bad times ahead, but I want to be there for the good, the bad, and everything in between."

"Brody, I love you, too! You're right, there's been something between us from the start. When Tessa introduced us, I felt something. It's hard to put into words, because it felt real and overwhelming and inevitable and I wasn't ready. Too much ugliness colored my world up until then, and seeing your face, it felt like the sun was finally shining again. Honestly, it scared me. Then I got to know you. Every day, when I'd see you, you always had a ready smile and a willing heart. It felt right—good—to call you a friend, but that friendship has evolved. It's grown into something so much more. Something I want to explore and share with you. I love you so much."

Brody pulled her against him, and Beth went on her tiptoes, twining her hands into his hair and pulled him close, pressing her lips against his. This, right here, right now, felt more right than anything ever had in her entire life. Being in Brody's arms, feeling the rush of emotions swamping her at his kiss, knowing the love she'd harbored for him was returned, made everything in her world shift on its axis until her life felt whole. With Brody, she had everything.

The kiss deepened in a sweet battle, and Beth wished this moment could last forever. If she could freeze one moment in time, to preserve it, cherish it, and hold onto it forever, it would be this one, knowing she was safe and secure in the arms of the man she adored.

Brody finally pulled back, and they were both out of breath. Beth looked at Brody's face and started chuckling. At his quizzical look, her laughter deepened, until she clutched her sides. Brody's smile grew at her hilarity, and she managed to finally stop laughing.

"What's so funny?"

"You do realize we've said we love each other, and want to spend the rest of our lives together, and we haven't even been on a single date?"

The sound of several people snickering wafted through the open windows, and Beth looked at Brody, and they both broke into peals of laughter.

"Guys, you're killing my moment here," Brody groused, though his voice was teasing.

"Hey, the folks interrupted when I was telling Tessa I loved her. No reason it shouldn't happen to you too." Rafe opened the door and walked out onto the porch. "Congratulations, Beth. All I can say is, it's about time you put the big jerk out of his misery."

"Bro, really, stop being a buzzkill."

"What? We caught the bad guy, saved the little damsel in distress, and you love the fairy princess. All-in-all, I think you've had a pretty good day. Now come inside before Momma has a stroke." He leaned in and whispered, "Be thankful I kept her inside as long as I did, or you'd have never been able to talk." With a wink, Rafe walked back inside.

"We've got a lot to work through, but I know we can get through anything, as long as we do it together."

Beth placed her hand in his. "Together. I like the sound of that."

"You know, you're a part of the Boudreau family and everything that goes along with it. You'll never be alone again."

Thinking about the huge, loving family Brody was part of, and how they'd raised him and stood beside him, made her and Jamie feel welcomed as their own, there was only one answer.

"I like the sound of that even better, Brody. Becoming a Boudreau—sounds perfect."

CHAPTER TWENTY-FIVE
EPILOGUE

Ridge leaned against the railing of the back patio, listening to the laughter from the people gathered out back. He'd missed out on all the excitement, not making it back in time to search for Jamie. But everything turned out fine, and it looked like he was going to get a new sister-in-law soon, if the way Brody and Beth kept making goo-goo eyes at each other was any indication. His brothers were falling for Cupid's arrow one by one. First Rafe, then Antonio, and now Brody. Shaking his head, he took a long drink from his bottle.

"Hey, bro. Heard you had a bit of excitement down on the border." Antonio walked over and perched on the porch railing. Ridge couldn't remember the last time his brother looked so—content. While he'd been living and working in Dallas, they'd managed to catch up several times a year, mostly when a case took him to the city to testify in a trial. Antonio had become more and more disenchanted with big city life. Now, he'd moved back to Shiloh Springs, found the perfect woman, and worked for the FBI out of their Austin office. The commute was long, but if it made his brother happy—more power to him.

"That bust was a long time coming. One point five million dollars' worth of cocaine off the streets, and we captured two of the upper level distributors. All-in-all, a good haul." He gestured with his drink toward Brody. "He looks happy."

"He is. Honestly, I'd been worried about him. When I first started working out of the Austin office, he seemed…withdrawn. Like the weight of the world sat on his shoulders. I knew something was up, but then I got dragged into the whole mess with Serena. By the time that got straightened out, he'd pretty much fallen for Beth. You know the rest."

"I know Stewart is back in Huntsville with a lifetime worth of charges against him. Think he'll take a plea again?"

"Chance is trying to see to it. He doesn't want Beth or Jamie to have to deal with all the fallout of a trial. Even if Stewart pleads guilty, he's looking at enough years added to his current sentence he'll be behind bars without the possibility of parole for the rest of his life." Antonio shook his head. "All because of money."

"Wonder why he couldn't accept Tessa and Beth gave the money from the bond back to Crowley County? All it would have taken was on phone call by his attorney, and it would have been proven." Ms. Patti motioned for them to come join the party, and he raised his bottle and nodded, letting her know they'd be there in a minute.

"I wish I'd been here to help. Sound like things got hairy. Poor kid. At least Stewart was decent enough not to hurt his own daughter."

"Rafe said it got a little dicey when they arrested him. Dude had a gun, and Dad was sitting across from him. Course you know our brother, he let several of Williamson's finest into the back of the Braum's, and they covered his back. He snuck up on Stewart and had him on the ground hogtied before the idiot knew what hit him."

"Rafe thinks he's Superman." Ridge smiled, remembering back to a Halloween when Rafe had actually dressed up as his favorite character.

"He's a bit more careful now he's got someone he loves in his life. Tessa's been good for him."

"Serena's been good for you too, bro."

Antonio grinned, leaning farther back on the railing. "I never thought I could feel this way. She's—everything to me. Everything."

Another wave of laughter came from the patio, and he watched his father flipping steaks and burgers on the grill. People mingled, holding paper plates and cups, or seated around the patio on the couches and chairs spread about. Today was a celebration of life and happiness. Brody and Beth had announced they were getting married, and he was going to adopt Jamie. Teasing and congratulations spread like wildfire throughout the gathering as people wished them well. Ridge hoped they'd make it for the long haul. If he was a betting man, he'd wager they'd make it.

Love and marriage? It wasn't for him. He believed in it—he'd grown up with the perfect example of true love lasting through the years. Douglas and Ms. Patti epitomized what love and devotion meant in the truest sense of the word. They'd opened their hearts, their family and their home to others in desperate need of salvation, sown the seeds of kindness, and raised a family, himself included, who knew what that meant in every way that counted.

But for him, the job came first. Before love. Before marriage.

He'd seen far too many people's lives destroyed by the onslaught of drugs crossing the border, to say nothing of the meth epidemic currently ravaging the nation. Besides, his job was dangerous, especially when he was undercover, which was more and more frequent these days. And it wouldn't be fair to get involved with somebody, only to be gone for weeks or months at a time. He risked his life every day, behind the scenes, dealing with the lowest of the low, the dregs of humanity who should be scraped off the surface of the planet, as far as he was concerned.

Nope, love and marriage weren't in the cards for him. Didn't mean he wasn't up for a good time. He loved women. All women. Big, small, short, or tall, didn't matter. Feminine curves with legs that went on for miles? Oh, yeah. But commitment for a lifetime—he'd never burden any woman with that kind of heartache. Turning his back on the war waging on every street in America couldn't be won without people like him staying the course. He wasn't a martyr, far from it, but he knew the realities of his life and his job.

"By the way, did you hear—Brody bought the Summers' farm."

Ridge knew his mouth hung open for a second before he closed it. He huffed out a chuckled. "Seriously? Why'd he do that?"

"He and Beth are going to fix up the house. Make it into a home. It wasn't damaged, and the rest of the property, other than the barn, is in decent shape. Lots of land."

"Almost seems like fate, doesn't it?" Ridge tossed his empty bottle into the recycling bin and grinned. "All's well that ends well. I'm just glad he's happy."

"Come on, bro, let's celebrate. We're all together, and life is good."

"You go ahead, I'll be right there."

As Antonio walked back to the patio, Ridge pulled out his phone. He'd put it on vibrate at the start of the barbeque, and he'd ignored the incessant buzzing, but couldn't put it off any longer. He knew who'd been calling anyway.

"Hey, boss, what's up?"

"We're a go."

A surge of adrenaline shot through Ridge at the man's words. Finally, they'd gotten the go ahead to search for the pipeline running through Central Texas. Every DEA agent within a two-hundred-mile radius knew drugs were coming through their area, but nobody had discovered exactly where the shipments deviated off their visual radar. He'd been scouting around an area the next county over from Shiloh Springs, and he'd gone to his boss with an idea—one so out-of-the-box he'd expected to be turned down on the spot. Instead, he'd listened, asked a zillion questions, and said he'd take it to his commander.

"We've got a very narrow window to find out how the drugs are moving through the area—if they are—and shut it down."

"I'll find it."

"I expect reports, consistent reports, every forty-eight hours. Miss one, and I'll pull you so fast, you'll leave skid marks. Are we clear, Boudreau?"

"Every forty-eight hours. I won't let you down."

"When can you head out?"

Ridge looked at his family, together and laughing, felt the gaping hole deep inside, and sighed.

"I'll head out tonight."

Disconnecting the call, he slid the phone into his back pocket, and smiled.

"Looks like I'm going courting."

Thank you for reading Brody, Book #3 in the Texas Boudreau Brotherhood series. I hope you enjoyed Brody and Beth's story. Want to find out more about *Ridge Boudreau and the excitement and adventure he's about to plunge headfirst into*? Keep reading for an excerpt from his book, *Ridge, Book #4 in the Texas Boudreau Brotherhood. Available at all major e-book and print vendors.*

Ridge (Book #4 Texas Boudreau Brotherhood series) ©
Kathy Ivan

Pulling into the garage, Maggie killed the engine and reached for the button to lower the door, but movement from the corner of her eye stopped her dead in her tracks. Somebody was sneaking around her property. Couldn't be Henry. She'd talked to him earlier that morning, and he'd asked for the day off. Felicia, her housekeeper, had already come and gone.

Reaching across the seat, she wrapped her hand around the shotgun and stepped out of the garage. Scowling at the thought of another trespasser, she skirted the perimeter of the house, eyes peeled for any sign of movement. *Nothing.*

Was her imagination playing tricks on her? She was getting antsy, because she'd caught a couple of up-to-no-good squatters on the back forty of her property, and chased them off. Why couldn't people mind their own business, and keep their noses out of hers?

There it was again. Somebody crept around the edge of her patio, although creeping might not be the best word. He really didn't slink or even trying to hide. The way he walked reminded her of one of the bigger jungle cats. A lion or maybe a panther, all smooth, controlled muscle, coiled and ready to pounce.

With a moue of disgust, she flattened her back against the Texas limestone of her house and watched. Waited. And wondered what game the stranger was up to. He was far enough away she couldn't get a good look at his face, but the rest of him was a feast of sensuality. From his predatory walk to his dark hair, he exuded an almost feral nature. A wildness she'd never imagined being attracted to—until now.

His gaze seemed to miss nothing, studying not only the house, but the grounds. The flowering rose bushes she'd lovingly planted so long ago, when she'd first gotten married and life had been simpler. In hindsight, she could recognize the irony of planting roses. Her life had been nothing but prickly thorns for so long, she'd all but forgotten there was beauty to go along with the pain.

Some instinct must have alerted him, though she hadn't moved a muscle, because he stopped, frozen in place. He spread his hands out to his sides, palms forward, showing them to be empty. She knew he hadn't spotted her, but something made him realize he wasn't alone.

Lifting the shotgun in front of her, she stepped out into the open, and pointed it straight at him. Never wincing. Never flinching.

"I don't know who you are, and I don't care. I've only got one thing to say." She hefted the gun higher, pointing it directly at his head. "Get off my property."

LINKS TO BUY RIDGE:

www.kathyivan.com/Ridge.html

NEWSLETTER SIGN UP

Don't want to miss out on any new books, contests, and free stuff? Sign up to get my newsletter. I promise not to spam you, and only send out notifications/e-mails whenever there's a new release or contest/giveaway. Follow the link and join today!

http://eepurl.com/baqdRX

REVIEWS ARE IMPORTANT!

People are always asking how they can help spread the word about my books. One of the best ways to do that is by word of mouth. Tell your friends about the books and recommend them. Share them on Goodreads. If you find a book or series or author you love – talk about it. Everybody loves to find out about new books and new-to-them authors, especially if somebody they know has read the book and loved it.

The next best thing is to write a review. Writing a review for a book does not have to be long or detailed. It can be as simple as saying "I loved the book."

I hope you enjoyed reading Brody, Texas Boudreau Brotherhood.

If you liked the story, I hope you'll consider leaving a review for the book at the vendor where you purchased it and at Goodreads. Reviews are the best way to spread the word to others looking for good books. It truly helps.

BOOKS BY KATHY IVAN

www.kathyivan.com/books.html

<u>TEXAS BOUDREAU BROTHERHOOD</u>
Rafe

Antonio

Brody

Ridge

<u>NEW ORLEANS CONNECTION SERIES</u>
Desperate Choices

Connor's Gamble

Relentless Pursuit

Ultimate Betrayal

Keeping Secrets

Sex, Lies and Apple Pies

Deadly Justice

Wicked Obsession

Hidden Agenda

Spies Like Us

Fatal Intentions

New Orleans Connection Series Box Set: Books 1-3

New Orleans Connection Series Box Set: Books 4-7

CAJUN CONNECTION SERIES
Saving Sarah
Saving Savannah
Saving Stephanie
Guarding Gabi

LOVIN' LAS VEGAS SERIES
It Happened In Vegas
Crazy Vegas Love
Marriage, Vegas Style
A Virgin In Vegas
Vegas, Baby!
Yours For The Holidays
Match Made In Vegas
One Night In Vegas
Last Chance In Vegas
Lovin' Las Vegas (box set books 1-3)

OTHER BOOKS BY KATHY IVAN
Second Chances (Destiny's Desire Book #1)
Losing Cassie (Destiny's Desire Book #2)

ABOUT THE AUTHOR

USA TODAY Bestselling author Kathy Ivan spent most of her life with her nose between the pages of a book. It didn't matter if the book was a paranormal romance, romantic suspense, action and adventure thrillers, sweet & spicy, or a sexy novella. Kathy turned her obsession with reading into the next logical step, writing.

Her books transport you to the sultry splendor of the French Quarter in New Orleans in her award-winning romantic suspense, or to Las Vegas in her contemporary romantic comedies. Kathy's new romantic suspense series features, Texas Boudreau Brotherhood, features alpha heroes in small town Texas. Gotta love those cowboys!

Kathy tells stories people can't get enough of; reuniting old loves, betrayal of trust, finding kidnapped children, psychics and sometimes even a ghost or two. But one thing they all have in common – love and a happily ever after).

More about Kathy and her books can be found at

WEBSITE: www.kathyivan.com

Follow Kathy on Facebook at
facebook.com/kathyivanauthor

Follow Kathy on Twitter at twitter.com/@kathyivan

Follow Kathy at BookBub
bookbub.com/profile/kathy-ivan